THE BOY BEHIND THE WALL

THE BOY BEHIND THE WALL

MAXIMILLIAN JONES

WELBECK
FLAME

Published in 2021 by Welbeck Flame
An Imprint of Welbeck Children's Limited,
part of Welbeck Publishing Group.
Based in London and Sydney.

www.welbeckpublishing.com

Text © Tibor Jones Studio Ltd

A CIP catalogue record for this book is available from the British Library

ISBN: 978-1-80130-000-1

Printed and bound by CPI Group (UK)

10 9 8 7 6 5 4 3

BERLIN, 1967

HARRY

I was swinging through the backstreets of the city on the lookout for trouble. I was new in town, but superheroes don't have to worry about being in strange new places. Some days I was Batman, some days Captain America, but on my way back from school that afternoon I was Spider-Man. I had just sent a gang of Commies scurrying for cover and was getting close to home.

Then the shouting started.

'*Halt! Sonst schießen wir!*' Words in German that I couldn't understand.

Then the gun-shots. Two in quick succession.

I looked up in time to see him slump across the top of the Wall. A slim boy with brown hair and green eyes. He looked a little like me. I saw him trapped eight feet above my head, snared in the barbed wire, blood blooming through his shirt.

He was still moving. I couldn't look away. He raised his head and seemed to look straight at me.

Heavy boots came running past me. An American soldier pushed me out of the way.

'*Verschwinde*,' he shouted in accented German.

This one I knew. 'Get out of here.'

But I couldn't move.

Then came the final shot.

Words were shouted across the Wall. More German words I didn't know.

It was the guards from the East that got to him first. The boy's left arm was caught on the top of the barbed wire and his legs were stuck beneath it. He was suspended above us like a puppet held up by strings. They tugged and tugged at him until finally he came free. I watched his body get dragged back over the Wall, finally disappearing back into the East.

The Americans relaxed, stopped aiming their guns. One of them turned to me and, bringing back his civilian smile, said, '*Wie heißt du?*'

'Harry,' I said, feeling faint. 'Harry Rogers.'

'How old are you?' He asked, switching to English.

'Thirteen.'

He put a hand on my shoulder and said, 'Well, Harry

Rogers, I'm sorry you had to see that. Are you going to be OK getting home?'

'I live just up the street,' I said, feeling stupid as I pointed vaguely in the direction of my apartment building, my hand trembling a little.

'Ok then, why don't you run on home now? Try not to think too much about it.'

It had only been three weeks since we arrived in Berlin, a divided city in a divided country. We had learnt a bit about Germany at school back in D.C., but I knew very little about the country before Dad accepted a placement here. One thing I did know was that it had been divided up by the Allies after the war. The Soviet Union took charge in the East, and the French, the British, and us Americans controlled various zones in the West. The weird thing is that although Berlin is actually in the East, the Allies split it up too. Supposedly, both East and West Germany are now sovereign states, which means they are in charge of themselves.

The Soviets are Communists. My dad says that means they think the government should run everything. They hate America because *we* believe individuals should be free and not have their lives decided by their leaders. That seems pretty strange to me, because who would hate freedom? I guess that's why millions of East German citizens started heading across the border. The Communists weren't happy about losing so many people, so, six years ago, in the summer of 1961, their leaders ordered the border be closed. First they put barbed-wire fences up, then they started construction on a huge concrete wall that stretches all the way around West Berlin. The *Vopos*, the East German police, guard it day and night to prevent people crossing illegally. It must have been them who shot the boy I saw.

I was only there that day because I had got lost again. Sometimes, when I'm feeling a bit nervous, I pretend to be one of the superheroes from my comic books. But even Spider-Man can find it tricky to navigate a new city. So I use the Wall as a landmark to help me find my way home from school. It's kind of weird how it just cuts through everything – a series of straight lines that divide streets and parks. There's even a house near our building with its front door in the West and its back door in the East; the family who lived there had to move out.

Our apartment is in the American Sector, where most of us expat Americans live, and is within sight of the Wall. I knew if I kept the Wall on my right it would always lead me back eventually. That's how I was where I was that afternoon, pretending to be Spider-Man ready to take on the world. Only, I wasn't ready. There was nothing I could do.

I was gasping for breath when I got back to the apartment and told my mom what had happened. She pulled me close to her, gripped me tighter than she had done in years, and we cried there in the kitchen together.

She made me hot chocolate.

'Drink this,' she said. 'It might help you feel better.'

'Mom, I'm not a kid any more,' I said, sounding like a scared child.

It was only when I took the cup that I realised my hands were still shaking. It didn't taste the same as back home, but she was right. It was comforting.

Later, in my bedroom, I tried to get the sight of the dead boy out of my mind. I tried to forget about the look in his eyes. I stared at the posters on my wall. All superheroes, like Iron Man and Hulk, Captain Marvel and The Thing. These characters had meant so much to me that morning, but now they seemed so childish.

I couldn't stop myself from looking out of my window. Our apartment was so close to the Wall that I could actually see into the East from my room. I'd never really thought about it before. About how strange that was. That these two worlds could be so close physically, but so separate, so different from each other.

Dad was late home from work that night. I was in bed by the time I heard the key scrape in the lock and the front door open and close. I was still awake. I hadn't been able to sleep. But I didn't want to have to face him, to explain everything and go through it all again. I heard muffled voices on the other side of my bedroom wall. Mom filling him in on what had happened. Their voices grew louder before falling quiet again. My door opened and the shaft of light from the hallway fell across my face. I pretended to sleep.

'Look at him. So precious,' said Mom.

Dad said nothing, just shut the door. He wasn't a man that often showed his emotions. Everything about him was closed.

In the morning, the three of us sat and ate breakfast. Bacon and scrambled eggs, with Mom serving up a larger portion than usual.

'How are you, son?' Dad asked.

'I'm fine,' I said, not looking up from my plate.

'He's not fine,' said Mom. 'And neither am I.'

Dad seemed about to reply but stopped himself. Instead, he downed the remains of his coffee and stood up. The door slammed shut as he left for work.

'I'm sorry,' Mom whispered, staring straight ahead. 'You know how stubborn he can get.'

In the days that followed the shooting, I tried my best to get back to normal life – or what was supposed to be normal now that we lived in West Berlin. Back home, I had actually enjoyed going to school. The only subject I was really any good at was maths, but it was worth sitting through boring Geography lessons because I also got to hang out with Mike and Robbie and throw a football around at lunch. I hadn't made many friends at my new school and, although we were all taught in English, I now found I couldn't concentrate in class. In the evenings, I tried to lose myself in listening to music or reading my comic books like I used to, but I kept thinking about the boy. I got goose bumps on my flesh when I thought about what he was running from, what he was prepared to risk his life for.

His face kept coming back to me as well. The sound of that final shot. I woke up in the dead of night, drenched in sweat.

Dad had raved about the American Sector before we came.

'It'll be just like home,' he said. 'They've got hot dogs and Twinkies and there's a Fourth of July parade. We'll fit right in, you'll see.'

Mom was doing her best now that we were here as well, despite taking every opportunity to point out issues to my dad. She was committed to recreating a little piece of D.C. in West Berlin. The rooms decorated to replicate what we were used to: a modern kitchen, a television set and a brand-new stereo. The wallpaper in the living room looked almost identical to what we'd had at home. But nothing was quite the same, and that included my parents.

I don't know if their problems had started before we left home, but they argued more and more these days, mostly when they thought I couldn't hear them. The arguments always started differently but ended with the same thing. Mom wanted to go home. Dad insisted we had to stay.

I didn't tell him I had started to run to and from school, too scared to stop anywhere in between. He didn't notice that at the weekends, I always stayed home.

Mom noticed though. And, although she was still wary about Berlin, she had decided that I shouldn't be afraid of our new home. She came up with excuses to send me out on errands. She'd make me go down to the laundromat. Or send me out to the grocery store for something she'd forgotten. A couple of weeks after the shooting, she decided she wanted ground beef. She said the stuff from the local store was too lean, so I had to head over to the butchers in Britz, about a thirty minute bike ride away. I knew the area a little because we had taken a family trip to an old manor house there about a week after we arrived. Still, it was further away from home than anywhere I'd gone alone since the shooting. The Wall loomed as I set out on my mission and I imagined all kinds of horrors playing out on the other side.

I had almost forgotten that the Electric Palace existed until I came across it again on my way to the butchers. It was weird discovering a cinema that played American movies, in English, in this foreign land. I had more than enough money in my pocket to pay for a ticket and still get the meat for Mom. I was sure she wouldn't mind if I caught a picture; she was the one that was always encouraging me to venture out, after all. The guy in the ticket office spoke good English and told me he'd keep an eye on my bike. I bought my ticket and settled down to watch Paul Newman in *Cool Hand Luke*. Newman plays a former soldier called Luke Jackson who is arrested and gets sent to work on a prison farm in Florida. Instead of keeping his head down and doing his time, Luke always stands up for himself even when the odds are against him. He even attempts to escape several times. For two hours, I couldn't take my eyes off the screen. I forgot about the world outside as I witnessed this hero not taking no for an answer.

By the time the movie was finished, it was dark outside and I'd completely forgotten about the shopping.

When I got home, Mom rushed to the door, worried because I had been gone so long.

'Are you OK? Did something happen?'

'No, sorry, Mom, I'm fine,' I told her, releasing myself from her embrace. And I really did feel better, as if a little of Luke's confidence in the movie had rubbed off on me.

In the following weeks I watched as many movies as I could, wiling away the hours after school. *A Fistful of Dollars*, *The Dirty Dozen*, stories about heroes – but not superheroes, real people who put themselves in the way of real danger.

I came out of the Electric Palace and imagined I was bullet-proof. I still found the Wall intimidating, but somehow, I felt less afraid. I started exploring again too. Discovering more of Berlin's jumble of streets still scarred by the war. New buildings sprouting like young trees from the charred soil after a forest fire.

Some days, after school, I would head down to watch the planes take off from Tempelhof. It was on one of those afternoons down by the airport that I discovered the comic-book store. It was an innocuous building between a bakery and a bank, all dusty and tired, with a door that creaked when you opened it. But inside it was vibrant, with splashes of colour from all the covers of the comic books. I remembered how much these books had meant to me back in D.C. I was drawn to them, although they were kind of childish. After what I'd seen, I knew I'd never feel really excited about comic books like these again.

'Good day to you,' said the old man behind the counter in heavily accented English. I don't know how he could tell I wasn't German. 'I am Dieter, the owner of this splendour. How may I help you today?'

Dieter moved very stiffly, but his eyes were alive and flickered with curiosity.

'Are you looking for anything in particular?' he asked again.

I hesitated, unsure. 'Do you have any American comics?'

'Aha, yes,' he said, shuffling down an aisle. 'What's your poison? *Der* Incredible Hulk? *Herr* Spider-Man?'

I went home with two new issues of *Superman* that day and started visiting Dieter's store on a regular basis after that. The cinema was great, but there weren't enough new movies to keep me busy and I sometimes felt silly sitting watching on my own.

Dieter always seemed pleased to see me, but never pushed me to talk. We'd sometimes spend hours in each other's company. I would read half a dozen comic books before buying one to take home with me, while he fussed around the shop or assisted the occasional customer.

Whilst a lot of the shop was given over to German comics, Dieter seemed most drawn to American culture. He would sometimes show me some of his old comic books, early versions of *Superman* and *Captain Marvel* from before the war. It was fascinating how they'd changed, the illustration styles becoming darker, more complex. He always had his radio tuned to American or British stations as well, listening to The Beach Boys, The Beatles and The Rolling Stones. He would dance robotically around the shop when no one else was around, even sometimes singing along. It was strange how spending time with him somehow reminded me of home.

JAKOB

There was a piece of classical music by the composer Bach that I was struggling to master on my violin. I remember Bach's Violin Sonata No. 1 from when I was very little. It was a piece my mother played over and over at one time, rehearsing for an important performance. Towards the end there is a sequence that I could never make to sound like it did when she played it. It's not really that tricky to play; the parts are easy enough to master with practice. But the whole thing seems to turn upon that section, like a door swinging on a hinge. The violinist must *feel* their way around this hinge. If the feeling is not there, the promise of the whole piece is never quite fulfilled. But if they do get it right, somehow the rest of it just opens up.

It was that section that I was struggling with, in my bedroom, one evening last September. Again and again, I repeated it, waiting for that moment I hoped would come, when it would feel as if the music was written in my fingers.

As if getting it right would somehow carry me back eight or so years to when I was five or six, before my life got ripped apart. But each time I played it, something was wrong – the tuning, the tempo, a note played a bit off-key or held a fraction too long. Then I would stop and reset my bow, start again from the beginning.

Some might assume that when I'm playing, I'm not aware of what is happening around me. The opposite is true. I am intensely aware of my surroundings. My senses are finely tuned.

Beneath the singing of the strings on my violin, I could hear the thrum of traffic, three storeys down, on Dimitroffstraße. I could hear the knocking on my bedroom door. I could see the daylight fading all over Berlin, East and West. I could smell the carrot stew that Margot had made.

Margot entered my room. Her eyes, lined with papery blue make-up, scanned the room and came to rest on a point just above my head.

'Dinner, Jakob. Your father is waiting.'

'Yes, Mother.' I hated calling her that. Margot and Hans had adopted me after my real parents were labelled traitors by the government. I loathed them, but I had found it was usually easier to play along with the sham.

Hans was at the head of the table. Margot and I sat either side of him. His grey eyes tracked me closely – a sign I should have picked up on. But I was distracted. In my mind's ear, I could still hear the melody of the music, rising and falling.

The stew in front of me was bright orange, with pieces of dark purple salami scattered through. After a first mouthful, peppery and sweet, I realised how hungry I was. Within a minute, I had cleared half my plate. Hans and Margot were picking at their food. Eventually, Hans laid down his fork and spoke.

'How was school today?'

I had a mouthful of food to finish before I could speak. All the time I was chewing and swallowing, Hans' gaze never wavered.

'It was very good, Father,' I managed to say after a pause. I forced a small smile, then lifted another forkful to my mouth.

Hans and Margot looked at each other.

'Tell me then, Jakob. What did you learn today?'

'Russian. Physics. Usual stuff. Nothing interesting.'

'Ah!' Hans nodded. 'Russian. Physics.' He looked down at his bowl, then carefully speared a cube of meat with his fork and lifted it to his mouth. He chewed the tiny morsel with a sideways, thoughtful expression.

'I always wished,' Hans said, 'that my Russian was better. Perhaps you could share a few Russian words with your mother and I that you learnt today at school.'

I could feel Margot's gaze flicking between the two of us, but I did not dare break Hans' stare.

'I ... well, let me fetch my textbook.' I wanted to stand up, but my legs did not budge.

'No need for that, surely, Jakob? It was only a few hours ago. It is important to try and remember things. It trains the memory. And one's memory can be so useful.' Hans tapped his temple and smiled.

I hadn't gone to my Russian class that day. I hadn't been at school at all.

And Hans knew that.

How had Hans known? I wondered. But then I remembered – this was Hans. Hans knew. It was his job to know.

I was cornered.

'I wasn't there today.'

Hans exhaled softly, but he didn't say anything, and I felt words bubble out of me. 'I ... I didn't feel well.'

Hans' palm slapped down hard on the table. Margot and I jumped in our chairs. She clutched her neck.

'There! Right there! You are lying again!'

My mouth opened and closed. I looked down at the half-eaten bowl of carrot stew. But as suddenly as Hans' explosion had come, it was gone. When he spoke next, his voice was low.

'Jakob. Your mother and I are concerned about you. Your exams are next year. You are not giving your education enough attention.'

'But ... but I was practising.' I felt a whine creep into my voice and hated myself. 'I have a recital next week.'

Hans set his jaw at this, but Margot spoke before him. 'You are fourteen years old, Jakob. We attended your *Jugendweihe*. Yet you still act like a child.'

I didn't want to argue with them. I didn't want to be having this conversation at all. In my mind, it was clear. How could violin come second to school? But I only had two more years and after that I would be free. I'd be done with school and there would be nothing to stop me from leaving.

Two more years ...

'I – I'm sorry,' I said. 'Mother, Father, I'm sorry.' I was surprised at how easily the apology came out.

It seemed to work, because Hans nodded. 'Yes. I believe you are. But apologies are not enough. You know, Jakob, you are very bright, very intelligent. You have much potential with your violin playing. But your results at school must match your musical ability. They are currently those of an average student.' Hans turned his palms upwards, warming up to his lecture. 'And it is not just your schoolwork. Your teachers have expressed ... concerns that you do not interact so well with your peers. I know it is early in your life. Perhaps you think these things don't matter. But even now, mistakes can affect your later career.'

I had wondered how long it would take Hans to get to my 'career'. I gritted my teeth as he continued. 'You are lucky enough to live in the German Democratic Republic. Our society, here, is based on democratic, socialist ideas – we are all equal and everyone is judged on their abilities. You cannot hope to stake your future on your family connections.'

There was something about the way he said 'family'. Was there a tiny sparkle in the corner of his eyes, a flicker of his eyebrow?

From nowhere, a quivering rage coursed through me.

'*Family*, Hans?' I spat. 'You are *not* my family!'

I shoved my chair back, toppling it, and fled the room. In my bedroom, I leaned against the door, trembling. I tried to remember some of the things my music teachers had taught me to prepare for a performance – steady breathing, open shoulders – but it did not ease my shaking. I lay down on my bed. I could hear Hans and Margot talking in low voices to each other. They sounded calmer than I'd imagined, though I couldn't make out their words. I realised after a minute or two that I was still hungry. But I would not give them the satisfaction of returning to the dinner table.

In moments like these, I have always turned to music. I put a record on. I owned seven. Hans and Margot were very strict about what records I was allowed. Six of my seven records were by well-known composers like Tchaikovsky and Shostakovich. But the seventh record they did not know about. I kept it in the bottom drawer of my dresser, hidden underneath folded layers of winter clothes, only brought out for moments of true need. I don't even know if it was legal to own such a record.

Duke Ellington.

Duke Ellington is fantastic. A jazz pianist from the Big Apple (that's what they call New York in the West, according to my friend Jürgen), who leads the most amazing band of musicians. The band knows the songs inside and out, which is how they're able to improvise so brilliantly, playing around with the tune, turning it inside out. Jazz somehow makes all my worries drift away.

I turned the volume on the record player right down and stuffed a blanket beneath the door to block the sound. If Hans or Margot heard Duke Ellington coming from my room, they'd probably assume I was listening to Western radio. I often tuned in to the music shows broadcast from the other side of Berlin when the apartment was empty, and I knew some kids at school who did as well. I think quite a few of their parents listened to the Western news broadcasts to hear what was happening over there (although I couldn't imagine Hans ever trying to tune in to Radio Free Berlin). Doing so was a lesser sin than actually owning an American jazz record, but I'd still be punished if I was caught. Especially after what had just happened at dinner.

Once I had placed the needle in the groove and heard the sweet chiming of the piano, the busy buzz of the trumpet, I no longer cared. I moved the speaker right up next to my pillow so I could play it very quietly. Then I put my hands behind my head, stared at the ceiling, and thought about what I would do when I could leave this apartment behind. When I could finally start living my life, listening to and playing whatever music I wanted. Free from the pressure to follow in Hans' footsteps.

At some point during the second side, I fell asleep.

I dreamt about them. My real parents, and Katrin, my sister. It was the same dream I always have.

We are sitting in our old ground floor apartment in Hellersdorf. Surrounding us are tottering bookcases stuffed full, with folios of sheet music wedged into any available corner. I am in the kitchen, looking through the window. It is a perfect summer's day – warm, with the lightest of breezes. My mother is playing her violin, but not the classical music she played professionally. Instead, she's playing something folky, jaunty almost, the melody turning gentle pirouettes.

Outside, Katrin is trying to do cartwheels with a friend. They are laughing and falling down, and starting again.

Father enters the room.

'They are coming,' he says.

'The children,' Mother says from the other room, her voice strangely carefree, the violin still singing sweetly.

'We should stay together,' I say.

But they act as if I have said nothing. They are both smiling.

Then the dream shifts. My father and I are on a train, alone in a carriage. He is looking out the window. I cannot see his face. The train isn't moving.

'Why isn't the train moving?' Father asks.

He turns to me. He is the colour of snow. He is terribly, terribly frightened. And now I am frightened too.

Tap, tap, tap.

Down the corridor, in the train. A rapping, knocking sound. Voices, though I cannot hear the words – hard voices, asking questions, receiving answers.

They are looking for us.

We need to run. I pull at my father, but he is so heavy. He is frozen in place.

'Someone must have seen us,' my father says.

Tap, tap, tap. Closer now.

'Father, we have to go,' I say. 'Come with me.'

But he has turned to ice. He shakes his head, incredibly slowly. Each fraction of movement seems to take an eternity, as if he were a clockwork toy expending the last of its energy.

Tap, tap, tap.

They are outside the door to our carriage. The glass in the door is frosted. I can see two silhouettes looming. One of them raises a hand.

Tap, tap, tap.

When I woke, the needle had reached the end of the record and was making a scratchy, repetitive noise as it tried to reset itself. I switched it off. It was two in the morning.

I remembered, like I did every time I had that dream. Father was dead – he had committed suicide in prison, according to Hans. Mother and my sister were in the West. At least, I assumed they were. I hadn't seen or heard from them for eight years, since the flight from the apartment in Hellersdorf. I tried to broach the subject once with Margot, but she shut me down. Hans, I didn't dare to ask. I knew only a little about what my parents' crimes were supposed to be. Something to do with a committee, 'counter-revolutionary activities', illegal printing. Were they guilty? I did not know.

My official parents were now Hans and Margot Eberhardt.

Hans Eberhardt, Deputy Executive Director at the Ministry for State Security.

The Stasi.

And I was supposed to be grateful to him for taking me in. I was 'lucky' that my case had crossed Hans' desk. That he had taken pity on the son of two traitors. I think he must have been involved in pursuing the case against my parents, although I can't be sure. And I have a memory of Margot from before my parents disappeared. At least, I can remember a woman very like her talking to my mother at one of my school recitals. I'm not sure how they could have known each other.

'They were going to send you to the orphanage,' as Hans never tired of reminding me. 'But I could see the potential in that little boy.'

Two more years, I told myself. Two more years until I graduate and can get a job, pay for my own place, maybe even find a way into the West.

And what exactly are you going to do? I heard a voice in my head ask me, but I ignored it.

Two more years.

The next morning, Hans came to speak to me. I didn't want to see him, but I knew, from long experience, that it was easier to go along with what he wanted than to disobey him directly. Things could always be worse. My adoptive parents were sticklers for the rules. Their favourite punishment was confiscation. Toys, books, records, radio – all had been taken from me at some point to make sure I did what I was told. At least I knew my violin was safe. The government was keen to promote classical music because our excellence in the area was evidence that we were better than the West.

I knew Hans was a powerful man. I had seen the way other people – neighbours, shopkeepers, my schoolmates' parents – acted around him. Always friendly, always smiling, but never close. Perhaps if others feared him, it would be sensible for me to show some respect.

He was not, after all, my real father.

'Come in,' I said.

His face had softened from the previous evening. He entered my room, inspected the sheet music on my stand. It was the Bach piece I had been playing the previous evening.

'You like this?' he said.

'Yes, very much.'

'What is it about it you like?'

I thought about this for a moment; I didn't want to mention Mother. 'I don't really know. It's like a machine. If you move one bit, the whole thing stops working. It is only perfect as it is. Do you understand?'

I had never seen Hans listen to music.

'Yes, I understand. It reminds me of the society we have here. So very precise. Everyone has their part to play, no matter how small. Even you, Jakob. Music is important. Culture is important. And we need musicians. But there are other things that matter, Jakob. You are young. It is not wise to put all your eggs in one basket. Am I making myself clear?'

'You are saying I shouldn't neglect my other studies.'

'Yes. But it's more than that. All your mother and I want

is for you to be the best you can be. To be fulfilled. This great country needs you. Young men of promise, who can help do the work that needs to be done. I want to offer you a deal. Do you remember the Funkhaus Studios?'

I blinked. Of course I remembered the Funkhaus Studios. Hans had an office there because the man who'd had his job before him had been a fan of the musical arts. Hans had kept the office because it was useful for him to have somewhere to go, away from the prying eyes of lower-ranked officials. In his line of work there were always people who wanted to find dirt on him. Something they could use to get him in trouble so that they could take his job.

In any case, it meant I had been allowed on a tour of the building with him once when I was eleven. I had memories of a great palace of steel and gold, huge concert halls, endless gleaming corridors. A jewel in the crown of the GDR. It was supposed to be the most advanced, the most modern, the most sophisticated recording studios in the whole world. We'd seen the world-renowned Berlin Symphonic Orchestra play and it had felt like I was flying.

'Yes,' I said, warily, 'I remember it.'

'Would you like to work there? I have a colleague who is an engineer. He would agree to teach you. You would get a chance to learn the arts of the recording studio. There are orchestras you could play in. Then you could see for yourself what the life of a musician is really like.' The way he said it suggested that once I found out, I might change my mind. But I didn't care.

'You would do this for me?'

'It would have to be outside of your school hours, of course. And there is a price. You will focus on your studies. If the reports from your school do not improve, I reserve the right to take this privilege away. You are aware it is a very great privilege?'

So it was a bribe. I knew it was a bribe. But, as much as I am ashamed to admit it, the temptation was too great. I had two years to get through before I could get a job and find a place of my own. I could pretend for that long. I could pretend to be the studious, model teenage citizen. And the Funkhaus! Just the thought of having access to that place made my heart leap.

'I understand.'

Hans nodded. A deal done.

'Very well, then.' He made to leave my bedroom, but he stood in the doorway and looked at me expectantly.

'Thank you ... Father.'

As soon as he left, I picked up the violin and played the

Bach sequence from beginning to end. The section I had worried about so much the previous evening was no longer a problem. I sailed through it, the music seeming to guide my fingers to play it perfectly.

But, when I finished, a black thought spoilt my pleasure. It took the shape of a smile – the tight smile on Hans' face as he left my room and shut the door quietly behind him.

He had offered the bribe and I had taken it.

HARRY

Things started to get back to normal as the days and the weeks went by. I'd started to feel a little safer going out again and was even beginning to think of this strange city as my home. The nights were still difficult though, and I wasn't sleeping well. My parents knew that. Some nights I would wake up screaming.

Mom tried to maintain some kind of routine, but she seemed distracted. Dad would try to talk to me sometimes, but he was so busy with everything in his job he didn't have much time. Perhaps that's why Mom was eager for me to get back to playing the piano. She needed a way to reach out and grab me and shake me back to my old self.

I was hiding out in my bedroom, reading issue 199 of *Superman*, one of the comic books I'd bought from Dieter. I'd just got to the part where a race had been arranged between Superman and The Flash, when I overheard Mom's voice coming from the living room.

'I wonder if music would help him, Walt. Remember how happy he was in his lessons back home? It might help him forget what he's seen.'

Dad had obviously agreed, because the next day Mom asked me to go and see him in his study. The room was stuffed with his books and papers, copies of the telegrams and letters that had brought us to Berlin and the files and folders that kept us there. He sat me down at the piano that had come with the apartment and asked me to play something. It took me a minute or so to get the hang of it again, but I was soon enjoying playing my favourite Elvis Presley song, 'All Shook Up'. My dad was obviously pleased too, because not long after that, he told me that he'd arranged for my lessons to start again.

I'd played piano back home, but for some reason I hadn't felt the urge to play since arriving in Berlin. I wasn't a bad pianist, although I struggled to read music. If I had to take lessons again, I hoped my teacher would be someone like Dieter – a German who loved life, who loved to laugh, who loved rock and roll.

But the wizened old guy my parents hired was nothing like Dieter. Herr Müller stood over me while I played, commenting bitterly on my every mistake. Worse still, he only ever wanted me to play the classics. He loved Brahms and Beethoven and would mutter darkly whenever I suggested we could play something else.

Sheet music. I mean – who needs it?

I would see the irritation in his eyes, under their overgrown brows, whenever I tripped up over some Beethoven piece. He seemed genuinely angry at my failure.

But when he left each week, shaking his head, I stayed on the stool and played with the freedom my lessons didn't allow. I'd try songs I'd heard on the radio. Songs like 'All You Need is Love' by a British band called The Beatles or 'Break on Through' by The Doors, working out the melody with my right hand. Playing these songs helped me forget about everything else that was going on. It was like how I used to feel reading comic books, like an escape from the world, at least for a little while.

Mom still desperately wanted us to go home. I could see how exasperated my dad got every time she mentioned it. His jaw would stiffen and he would fall silent whenever she made one of her comments. But that didn't stop her bringing up how difficult life was here, especially for me, after what I'd seen. A couple of times he cracked and an argument ensued. Afterwards, my mom would disappear into their bedroom, and my father would lock himself in his office.

I played piano whenever I could. I was trying to fill the apartment with music. I imagined the notes drifting through the rooms, reaching my parents and bringing them together again like they used to be at home.

And one night, miraculously, it worked.

It was after dinner. The dishes had been cleared. My dad went to his chair to drink his bourbon and read the news. My mother sat opposite him, busying herself with the sewing of a button that had fallen from a blouse.

They forgot to ask me about any homework I had. They didn't notice me sneak off to the study.

I opened the piano and played a few tentative notes. A tune by the jazz singer Nat King Cole that I'd remembered.

It only took a few bars for her to stop sewing. I could see her through the study door and down the hallway – a narrow view to her chair in the living room. She looked up, smiled in my direction, and then looked across at my dad.

'Oh, Walt,' she said, sighing. 'Do you remember this?'

I couldn't see my dad from where I was, but I could hear him.

'Baxter Ballroom, 1947. You were the most beautiful girl in the room.'

I wasn't expecting what happened next, and it almost made me fall off my stool.

Dad set aside his drink, tossed the newspaper to the floor, stood up, and asked Mom to dance. She laughed him off at first.

'Don't be silly,' she said.

She waved him away when he approached her chair.

'Walt, we're not a couple of lovebirds any more.'

But Dad wasn't taking no for answer, and soon my mom gave in and got up and they moved their feet together and swayed. They held each other close, moving in and out of my view, dancing to the rhythm of my playing.

There was a party the night we left America. A barbecue in our backyard in D.C. on a hot summer's evening. All of our family and friends were there. My mom moved through it all with drinks trays and food, making sure everyone was cared for. She played along with excitement when people talked about the 'adventure' we were going on.

Dad's career had been improving quickly, which was why we'd moved from Philadelphia to Washington a couple of years previously. When we arrived at the new house, Dad picked up my mom and carried her over the threshold, as if they were newlyweds. She screamed for him to put her down until they collapsed in a heap on the sofa, laughing and wriggling together.

The next day, he took me to Pennsylvania Avenue and we stared out together at the White House.

'Will you be president one day?' I asked him. I was young then, I meant it.

Dad looked down at me, smiled, rubbed my head and said, 'Now, that really would be something, wouldn't it?'

I didn't mind Washington. I missed my friends and family in Philly, but I made new friends like Mike and Robbie. And Mom had lots of friends there too. Then he got offered this important job in Germany. So we moved to Berlin.

It was raining when we arrived. A taxi took us down drenched streets that looked sorry for themselves, until we arrived at our apartment, the ugly brown block that was now to be our home.

My father began his speech before we had even set our bags down. He took us to the window and pointed down at the Wall.

'That's why we're here,' he said. 'Those damn Commies and their damn wall.' And then he went on with his familiar routine about honour and democracy. About freedom. The way he spoke about it, there was something inhuman about living in the East. The East Germans were brainwashed, told how to behave by the state. But not everything he said made sense to me. If Communism was bad, then surely a wall dividing East from West must be a good thing? It would keep *the disease of Communism* out. Maybe what annoyed him was that it was the other side that had put it up. Still, once I'd seen the Wall for myself, I had to agree with him that it didn't seem like a good thing. It cast a shadow over Berlin that made life here feel like living without proper sunlight. Thinking about it sent a shiver down my spine.

In the study, at the piano, I'd finished playing 'Unforgettable' by Nat King Cole. My parents were still dancing in the living room.

'Play another one, son,' I heard my dad call.

Mom laughed. It was the first time I'd heard her do that in at least a week.

'Walt, what's gotten into you?'

I worked up 'Save the Last Dance for Me' and watched them glide some more. Mom, in the arms of Dad, looked up and he kissed the top of her head. I was coming to the end of the song when the phone began to ring.

'Don't answer it,' Mom said. 'Whatever it is, it can wait until morning.'

'How about this one, Dad?' I said, and I banged out the opening chords to 'The Star-Spangled Banner,' expecting him to smile or cheer or sweep my mother off her feet. But he rushed to the phone and told us all to be quiet.

I carried on playing.

He said something quickly to whoever was on the other end of the phone. Then, leaving the receiver on the phone table, he stormed into the study and slammed the piano lid down, narrowly missing my fingers.

'I said, stop that,' he said quietly. Then he went back to the phone in the hall.

I froze for a moment at the piano. It was all going so well; it had almost felt like the old days – what had gone wrong?

I couldn't take it, I just wanted to get the hell out of there. I got up from the piano, rushed past Dad in the hall and ran out the front door. I raced down the flight of stairs and out into the Berlin twilight, and just kept going.

The only place I could think to go to was Dieter's store. It wasn't open, of course, but I could see a light on and Dieter was still pottering around near the back. He came to the door when I knocked and ushered me in.

'Are you OK, my friend?' he asked. 'Why are you out of breath?'

'I'm sorry,' I said, only then realising how silly it was for me to have just turned up like this at the door of a man who hardly knew me. 'I just needed to talk to someone and I couldn't think of anyone else.'

'Come, follow me.'

He led me down a short hallway behind the till that opened on to his living space, which I had never seen before.

There was a brown armchair and a lamp, an old television set and a bed in the corner. There was a stove, a sink and very little else. One door led to a tiny bathroom and another led out on to a small yard.

'I'm sorry, it's not much,' he said. 'Out there, the comics, the shop – that is my world. This is just a place for eating and sleeping in.'

Dieter busied himself at the stove, making us both a hot chocolate. It wasn't as good as my mom's, who always made it with milk, but I was grateful just the same.

'Now, what is it that's bothering you?' he asked, perching on a tired footstool so that I could have the armchair. And I don't know why, but I just found myself telling him about everything. About how my mom and I had never wanted to come to Germany, but we had to, for my dad's work. And about how distant he'd been since we arrived, and how hard I'd found it to settle in. I even told him briefly about what I'd seen, about the boy being shot.

'And then, tonight,' I finished, trying to stop myself from sobbing. 'Everything seemed to be going so well. It was like the old days, with Mom and Dad getting on again. Dancing together. And then, well, he just flipped.'

'I am sorry, Harry, that you have had to deal with all this at such a young age. I never got on with my own father either. A hard man, you know. Prone to outbursts like your own. I do not have any answers for you. But my little store is always open if you need somewhere to go.'

'Thank you,' I said, my voice barely a whisper.

'It's strange,' he continued. 'For years, I hated my father, but still, I miss him. Both of my parents died before the war.'

'I'm sorry,' I said.

'No, don't be sorry, it was for the best. My father, he fought in the first Great War. I think he never quite got over it. I'm glad he didn't have to face another.'

'What was Berlin like back then?' I asked. 'During the Second World War, I mean.'

'Dark, dark days,' he said, shaking his head and looking away. 'It was hard everywhere during the war. I think it is difficult for you Americans to understand. It was all a little distant for you, happening somewhere else. Until Pearl Harbour, I mean. But here, the war was everywhere. It touched everyone.

'I have not told many people this, Harry, and at one time it would maybe have been enough to get me killed, but I am a quarter Jewish. My grandmother on my father's side. She wasn't practising, not after she married my grandfather, anyway – he was Lutheran – so it was never really part of our identity until suddenly we had to hide it. What they did to the Jews during the war, Harry – people pretended not to know, but we all heard the rumours. It was almost a relief when I got called up to the army. At least I didn't have to witness what they were doing to my friends and neighbours.

'But this is not a conversation for now.' His face brightened as he changed the topic. 'I embrace today. That is the important thing. Live for the now. There is so much good in the world. There is suffering now in the East. Many of my friends did not manage to escape before the Wall went up. They write to me sometimes. They have to be careful, of course – letters are read at the border. But I can tell things are not so good there. And it hurts to be separated like this. But one day, East and West Germany will be reunited. I believe it. Maybe not in my lifetime, but in yours? I hope so.'

When I returned to the apartment, my parents had retreated to their corners. My father had locked himself in the study to deal with whatever the phone call had brought and my mother was over by the window, smoking a cigarette.

'Where did you go?'

'Doesn't matter.'

'Are you okay?' she asked me. 'I am sorry about your father, he's under a lot of stress.'

I put my arm around Mom's shoulders. She thanked me for the songs.

We watched a plane take off from Tempelhof, lights blinking like shooting stars.

'We'll be okay, won't we, Mom?'

She sighed as she blew out smoke. She stubbed her cigarette on the outside sill, and said, 'I'm really not sure any more.'

I paused, unsure how to respond. She had always put on a brave face for me before, even if I could see right through it.

'We'll get home, someday,' I said, trying to give my voice some authority. I hoped it would be soon.

I started spending even more time with Dieter at the comic-book store. He seemed to like having me around and I enjoyed being somewhere I was wanted. I must have spent hours leafing through all the comics.

Once or twice, I got talking to a couple of the other boys who came by to pick up the latest *Superman* or *Spider-Man*, but mostly it was Dieter that I went to see. He started lending me records too, stuff imported from America and the UK that wasn't available in many places yet. Bands with weird names like The Kinks or The Who or The Grateful Dead. He knew loads about British and American culture, and his English was so good that it made me embarrassed that my German was hardly improving at all.

Whilst the store felt more like home to me than our apartment, the comic books themselves seemed to be losing their power. Flicking through the latest issues of my old favourites, I began to have the same feeling I had about the posters in my room. There was something empty and childish about it all. Instead of immersing myself in some new adventure, I'd find myself thinking about that boy on the Wall again. Dieter hadn't told me all that much about what life was like over there, but I knew it must be pretty bad for people to risk their lives to escape.

About a week after my evening visit, Dieter noticed that I'd been browsing for half an hour and not settled down to read anything.

'Can't find anything you're interested in?' he asked, shuffling off his stool and stepping out from behind the counter. 'Come, my friend,' he said, leading me once more into that little back room he called his home.

He knelt and unscrewed the front of what looked like a pre-war television, the sort that only showed programmes in black and white. Instead of the jumble of wires and components I expected to see, I was surprised when he took out a pile of comic books.

'Here,' said Dieter, and he handed me a copy of *The Fly*. 'Not many people know about this one.'

The Fly was a spy comic, printed on an underground press in East Germany. It was about a German-American agent working against the East German government. Dieter told me that over the last ten years or so there had only ever been a dozen editions produced, and he had managed to collect about half of them. 'The Fly' was the code name for Jan Jäger, a troubled hero who could find a way out of any situation.

The cover showed The Fly etched in grey, wearing a long coat and fedora hat. He was leaning on a lamp-post by a wall in the rain, the end of his lit cigarette the only dash of colour in the picture. I had never seen anything like it. I was transfixed at the thought that there was a comic set so close to where I was living now.

'How much is it?' I asked, fumbling for change.

Dieter shook his head. 'This one is not for sale,' he said. He put his hand on top of mine and squeezed it. 'This is yours to keep. You are a stranger here. This might help you. But keep it to yourself, you understand? The Fly might be fighting against the East, but he is not exactly a fan of the West either. Some people don't like the world to be as complicated as this.'

He flicked through the book to a page that was taken up by a single panel. It showed people trying to get over the Wall. I knew he was showing me this panel because he knew what I'd seen.

'You see,' he said, putting the comic in a bag and handing it to me, 'this is art imitating life.'

The Fly had foiled the Stasi and marched these people to freedom. I had heard of the Stasi, but when I'd asked my father about them, he'd given only a very vague response.

'You don't need to worry yourself with that kind of thing,' he said. 'They are the kind of men I'm here to protect us against.'

I wondered what he meant by 'us', because I certainly didn't feel very protected here.

When I asked Dieter the same question, he looked at me, put both hands on my shoulders and said, 'The Stasi are the worst. They are state security for the government over there. But they hate their own people. I think many of them must hate themselves. And they are everywhere. They infiltrate every aspect of life in the East. You are never safe if you criticise the Government, but you are never safe even if you do not criticise the Government. Some people will always be willing to inform on you unfairly to gain favour with the higher-ups, or simply because they do not like you. And the Stasi will always believe the worst.

'Over there, you know – that is my real home. I was born outside of Berlin, in what is now part of the East. Over there, people can just disappear. Poof! And you never see them again. My brother, I haven't heard from him in a long time. But I can't ask questions. Nobody can ask those kinds of questions in the East. Or they just disappear too. This is why we must be – how do you say? – discreet. Be careful with that comic, Harry. It is not something to show around at school; not everyone shares our taste in reading material.'

'I will,' I said, grateful that Dieter would trust me with something like this. I was curious to know more about what life was like in the East but I hesitated before asking, unsure if Dieter would want to talk about it.

'What is it like over there? How else is it different to the West?'

'Oh, in some ways it is not so different from here.' Dieter looked out the window as he spoke to me. 'There is less choice, of course. There are no comic-book stores like this one for children to spend their pocket money in, although many of the people don't have enough to live on, so most of the children don't have pocket money anyway.'

I was suddenly conscious of the pocketful of change from the money my mom had given me.

'In some ways it feels a lot like during the war,' Dieter continued. 'Except not everyone suffers these days. The people at the bottom suffer, of course. But the people at the top don't suffer so much. It is those in charge there that are the real problem. They have taken a good idea and turned it into a bad thing. Selfishness and fear – that is what is destroying my homeland. Men who want to feel important and men who are scared what will happen if they let power slip.'

'A good idea – what do you mean?'

'The GDR calls itself a Soviet state. It's allied to the Soviet Union, a group of nations built on socialist principles of sharing more equally, with everyone contributing what they can and taking only what they need – that sounds all right, doesn't it? Well, maybe not to an American, but for some of us it used to seem like a good thing.'

'Are Communism and socialism the same thing?'

'Ah, now there is a question. Mostly it is you Americans who talk about "Communism" – we from the East prefer "socialism". They are similar, yes. Although, under Communism, the state dictates everything and the people own nothing for themselves. With socialism, there is supposed to be democracy. The people are supposed to have a say and be able to vote for their government, but that is not always how it works out.'

'My dad doesn't like socialism. He believes in freedom and that you should be free to own as much as you want.'

'Does he indeed? It's an interesting idea, of course, but I'm not sure that's a kind of freedom I would like. Personally, I quite like the idea of socialism. Each person doing their best to help the whole community. Everyone sharing equally in the benefits of that hard work. Unfortunately, that is not what happens in the East. Maybe it is not a thing that can ever really happen.'

'Why not?'

'I'm afraid, Harry, the men in charge have all but destroyed everything we were trying to build. Sometimes I wonder what we could have done differently. If there was a way of preventing those with the fewest morals from rising to the top.' He shook his head sadly. 'And now they maintain their power by sowing mistrust. By turning the people against each other, comrade on comrade, brother on brother.' His eyes had grown moist.

'I'm sorry, Harry. That was probably not what you were asking. But it pains me still, thinking of what might have been. Still, we are here now, and that is worth celebrating.'

I couldn't understand why he was still willing to defend socialism, when it was the reason his country was suffering now. But, listening to him speak, I realised that there was probably a lot I didn't understand.

That night I stayed up late reading, taking in every panel of *The Fly*. I examined every splash of colour, mouthed the words in speech blocks and wished I were among its pages, absorbed in Jan Jäger's world. I had never seen anything like it. The artwork was beautiful and dark. The story felt real. Like I was looking into the East. Dieter's East, the world he had had to leave. It made me want to do something to help, to reach out to those on the other side of the Wall. In the morning I stowed the comic book carefully under my mattress before heading to school.

We were doing a science project in class, investigating lighter-than-air gases. The teacher walked around the classroom dropping an uninflated balloon on to each of our desks. The English boy who sat next to me flicked his balloon at the girl in front. When she turned round, he looked accusingly at me as if I had done it. She didn't say anything, just frowned and turned back to her own desk.

School in Berlin was a place where expat kids were shoved into rooms and expected to muddle along. But even in this thrown-together group, I was somehow an outsider. I arrived mid-way through the semester, so friendship groups had already been agreed upon. Gangs formed. Not that I cared. Most of the kids were fond of gossip and stupid things that didn't matter to me. But I knew there were others like me, just waiting for whatever business our parents had here to be done, so that we could go home, to the country where we belonged.

In science class we lined up with our balloons and the teacher filled them all with helium from a tank. We then spent ten minutes tying little weights to the balloons. The idea was to find the smallest amount of weight required to keep the balloon from floating away. There was a formula to use to calculate the buoyancy force of the gas inside.

When break-time came, I didn't join the others breathing in the gas from their balloons and laughing at the effect it had on their voices. I had already decided what I was going to do. When no one was looking, I hid the full balloon in my bag to smuggle it home. It was a crazy plan, but for the first time in a long time, I didn't feel afraid.

Back in my bedroom, I hastily wrote out two postcards from the pile my mother had picked up to send home. I attached them to the balloon with a small piece of tape.

On the first card I scribbled, *Freedom will save the day, I promise. Hold on and keep believing.* On the second I just wrote my return address.

I opened my window and put my hand out into the cool evening air, trying to gauge the direction of the wind. Then I just let the balloon go. It was thrilling to watch it float high and be taken by the wind to drift miraculously over the Wall.

Then I heard the crack of a gun-shot and saw the balloon burst and fall from the sky.

JAKOB

At the Funkhaus, Hans introduced me to a man named Karl-Erich Christian, whose showy friendliness switched to a stiff wariness the instant Hans left me alone with him. As quick as he could, Herr Christian fobbed me off to a chain-smoking broadcast and recording engineer called Andi, who let me tag along behind him without ever getting too close. Perhaps he, too, was afraid of my adoptive father.

I didn't care.

I was allowed to spend Monday and Thursday evenings at the Funkhaus, and to me, everything about it was heaven. The gold-and-white corridors were lined with mysterious doors. One might open to a hushed little recording studio, with a million dials and switches and meters whose function I didn't know. Another door would lead to one of the gleaming white practice rooms, where the pianos were always in tune. Best of all were the few doors that led into a shining auditorium. There, you might find two hundred people talking in excited whispers, waiting for one of the many orchestras to fill the space with their music.

I wanted to absorb everything.

Andi didn't bother trying to teach me much about recording, but he let me watch what he did, and I began to learn what each of those dials was for. After a time, I drifted from Andi to other recording engineers, other musicians. There was a sense of community at the Funkhaus, an almost-family of comradely musicians – and I loved it.

Although I wanted to spend as much time as possible at the Funkhaus, I was aware of my promise to the Eberhardts about my schoolwork. I knew that they had not forgotten it either. I noticed Margot, when she thought I wasn't looking, scribbling in a little blue notebook that she pulled from her pocket when I left for school or when I got back from the Funkhaus.

'What are you writing?' I asked her, once.

'Shopping list,' she replied.

It must have been obvious to my adoptive parents how much I loved the Funkhaus. I am sure Herr Christian gave Hans reports on what I was working on, who I spoke to, how much I threw myself into it. Again, I didn't care.

At first, I thought that hard work at school would be

enough to placate them. Was I as bright as Hans made out? I didn't think so. I found it hard to concentrate in lessons. Chalked mathematical symbols would squiggle before my eyes and transform into music notes. When our English teacher read out phrases that the class was supposed to repeat – *Could you direct me to the train station?... Two hundred metres straight ahead, then turn right* – I found myself listening to her voice and wondering what key it was in.

After a few weeks of more or less aimless joy, wandering the halls of the Funkhaus, I applied to play violin in the Third Junior Orchestra. I wasn't sure how Hans would react when I mentioned this at home, but he seemed pleased that I was taking things so seriously. Besides, so long as my grades were still good I doubted he would complain.

The orchestra practised weekly. We played standard orchestral pieces by composers like Beethoven, Mozart and Strauss. But our conductor, a quiet woman in her fifties, also had a surprising taste for modern music. She would make us warm up with big-band jazz tunes from the forties, or musical songs from Broadway composers like the American George Gershwin. I always felt a bit guilty playing this kind of music; there was something not entirely socialist about it. I would refrain from practising at home when Hans and Margot were in.

I was now spending three evenings a week at the Funkhaus, lost in its musical wonderland, and practising the other evenings. I had to try to cram my schoolwork into any spare moment I could find.

It worked for a time, but inevitably, I slipped up.

We had a geography exam on the subject of 'the evolution of modern agricultural techniques'. Our teacher would spring these surprise tests on us. She would write a subject on the board and we would spend the entire hour of the lesson composing an essay on it. We weren't allowed books but we were expected to have done the reading she had set.

Of course, I hadn't.

I'd meant to. But somewhere between practice and Funkhaus and keeping up with physics and German and history, I had forgotten.

I had nothing to write.

I stared at the clock, then at the blank page, then back at the clock. Five minutes stretched to fifteen, and still the page was blank. In the end, I pretended I had an upset stomach and begged to go home.

Word of my 'illness' reached my adoptive parents. They were not outwardly suspicious, but Margot only let me eat dry toast for two days. They also forbade me from going to that Tuesday's orchestra practice.

'You don't look well enough,' Margot said, and I faked a weak nod and kept my annoyance hidden.

I realised then that I couldn't manage both my schoolwork and music. I knew that if I made a slip-up like this again, there was every chance I would be stopped from visiting the Funkhaus. But I would not give up on music. I needed to try a different approach.

I did not have many friends at school, as my teachers had noted. I felt different and I did not particularly seek people out. I had a reputation for strangeness too, and no doubt everyone knew about my family history. But last year, I had made one friend. His name was Jürgen Modrow.

Jürgen's father worked in the same division as Hans, but at a lower level. I was vaguely aware of this, but one day Jürgen had approached me as we left school together.

'My father wants me to make friends with you.'

'Why would he want that?' I said, but Jürgen just laughed.

'You know why, Jakob.' He pulled a funny, mocking face, crossing his eyes. I instantly liked him.

'Well, I don't know what your father thinks I'll be able to tell you. My father doesn't tell me anything interesting.'

'Mine does!' Jürgen affected a self-important tone. '"You'll never guess what I learnt today at work about Ulbricht!"' Ulbricht was the General Secretary of our Central Committee, so I was shocked that Jürgen's father would be so free with what he discussed with him. Jürgen just rolled his eyes. 'Besides, I don't think my father cares. It's something to tell the others in the canteen at work, that's all.' And he puffed his cheeks out again in that comical fashion. '"My son and Eberhardt's son, you know. Best of friends."'

After that, Jürgen was the closest thing I had to a friend. We weren't best friends; I never shared secrets with him, or told him about my real family. But he was someone to eat lunch with, to walk to and from school with. He regularly topped the teacher's list for Russian, and in mathematics and physics he was far better than anyone else. So it was him I turned to for help with my schoolwork. I arranged to spend spare evenings and weekend afternoons at his place, where he'd talk me through the homework and then I'd exchange niceties with his father. *An exchange*, Jürgen called it, and though to me it didn't feel like it, I suppose that's what it was.

It seemed to do the trick too. My schoolwork improved, Hans and Margot were satisfied, and I was free to spend those delicious, too-short evenings at the Funkhaus.

It was during one such evening that I met Dana.

It was impossible to miss Dana Decker. First Double Bass in the Third Philharmonic and didn't everyone know it? Always on time, always well rehearsed. She kept her black hair cut short and wore thick-rimmed spectacles over which she would stare disapprovingly if anyone made a mistake. She, of course, never made mistakes. One time, I even heard her tut when our band leader suggested we play 'Over the Rainbow' as a warm-up. She still played it faultlessly though.

She approached me after practice.

'Comrade,' she said, and bobbed her head. *Comrade*. 'You're Jakob Eberhardt, aren't you?' Of course she knew my surname. That must be why she was talking to me.

I nodded back at her, trying to appear uninterested.

'I've noticed you around.'

'Well, we do play in the same orchestra.' I zipped my violin case shut.

Dana blinked at me. 'Are you being sarcastic, comrade?'

I looked up then to see she was smirking a little. I felt the heat rise in my face, perhaps I had been too short with her. Whilst she was young enough to be in the junior orchestra, she was at least a couple of years older than me. She was also a Funkhaus regular, while I was still considered new. It would be wise for me to be more polite.

'Not sarcasm. Just tired.' It was true. 'You're Dana, right?' I smiled to seem friendly, but she continued watching me coolly behind those severe spectacles.

'Yes,' she said. 'I like your playing.'

I was a little taken aback. 'Thanks, I noticed you playing too. You're very good.' It was true – she wasn't just a faultless player, she seemed to come alive when she played. She was better than some of the double bass players I'd seen playing with the First Philharmonic. There was a kind of otherworldliness to her precision. I could feel myself getting a little flustered. 'Sorry, but I really must get home. My parents are expecting me.'

At the mention of my parents, as was so often the case, there was a tightening about her face. She knew who my father was. I felt a twinge of disappointment.

To me, the Funkhaus represented the pure joy of music, a love of sound, of melody. Though I knew the Funkhaus was regarded as a national treasure – it was frequently mentioned in the newspapers – I had managed to pretend to myself that somehow the place was above politics. But of course it wasn't. And Dana's reaction to a mention of my father brought that home to me.

It reminded me of something about myself too. Nowhere could I be just Jakob the violinist, or, God forbid, Jakob *Fiedler*. I was always Jakob *Eberhardt*.

But what Dana said next surprised me.

'This is not the only music I play. Have you heard of Café Bruno?' I shook my head. 'It's a small place, on Friedrichstraße. I play in a band there. We need a violinist.'

A band? A real live band.

'What kind of music?'

'Jazz, bossa nova. Different styles.'

I remembered that tut she had given. 'I thought you ...' But I didn't complete the sentence. I didn't want her to think I disagreed with her opinions on our conductor's musical choices. 'Why are you asking me?'

She fiddled with a button on her cardigan. 'As I say, we need a violinist. I've seen you play and I think you might have something. You could be a good fit.'

I didn't believe her, I wasn't even First Violin, why would she ask me? This was another deal. I was a route to my father. But the thought of playing with her in a band, a real live band, seemed so exciting, so bohemian. I envisaged myself on stage in a smoky café, bleeding my heart out on my violin, then the soft applause of the audience.

To my surprise, I was willing to trade.

When I got home, Hans and Margot were sitting in the living room, watching the television. I knew I wouldn't be able to keep it secret, so I told them about Dana's offer.

Hans shook his head a little, in obvious disappointment.

'Your schoolwork will suffer, Jakob, do you not think?'

'My marks have improved though, Father. Haven't my teachers said so?'

Hans could not disagree. Still, he looked doubtful.

Unexpectedly, help came from Margot. She turned her face away from the flickering screen and spoke softly. 'Perhaps he is *meant* to be a musician, Hans.'

I *am* a musician, I wanted to say.

'*Meant to be* ... I cannot deal in *meant to be*s.' Hans' mouth twisted a little. 'This Café Bruno ... you know what goes on in these places. People talk ... dangerous talk.'

'I don't think this café is like that, Father. I don't think Dana is like that at all.' An idea struck me. 'And if it is, well, would it not be better if you knew?'

Hans looked at me curiously. He was silent for a few moments. 'Very well, Jakob. But I want to meet this Dana for myself.' He exhaled through his teeth, raised his eyebrows. 'You and your mother are a formidable team!'

The meeting between Hans and Dana was arranged for the following week after orchestra practice.

I didn't warn Dana that Hans was coming beforehand. I told myself that it was because there hadn't been time before rehearsal, but of course there had been. I think now that I wanted to test her – to see how she would react.

Hans told me that he would arrive at eight when practice finished, but he turned up fifteen minutes before that. It wasn't unusual for people to enter and leave orchestra practice. Musical directors and talent scouts would sometimes sit high up in the stalls. Musicians from around the place would often come in to see what the other performers were doing. But when Hans entered, there was a distinct wobble in our music. Eyes turned to look at him, instruments slightly lowered. Those unblinking grey eyes gave off a kind of animal power that others instinctively noticed. Did the conductor speed up a little? I thought so, but I couldn't be sure – we were starting the climax of the symphony and there was a tricky bit that required my concentration. I forgot about Hans as I lost myself in the see-saw swirl of the orchestra.

As the echoes of the final notes drifted away, I looked over at Hans. Dana was already up and shaking his hand. I hurried to pack up my violin. By the time I reached them, they were mid-conversation. Hans smiled as I approached, but Dana's gaze remained cold.

'Here he is, finally! Are you sure your band needs someone whose head is always in the clouds, Miss Decker?'

She laughed. 'We will whip him into shape, Mr Eberhardt, don't worry.'

Hans grinned. 'Jakob, your playing today was beautiful.' He said it as if he really meant it, though I did not believe he knew the first thing about music. I wasn't sure he even *liked* music.

He turned back to Dana and fixed her with those grey eyes. 'You are a musician?'

'I want to teach music, comrade. I hope to apply for teacher training college next year.'

Hans nodded but said nothing.

Dana watched him in silence for a second, then continued, 'I think music has such an important role to play in our society. So often the propaganda we hear from the West, the story that they tell the public in their newspapers and on television, is that our lives are dull and plain. But look around.' She waved her hand to emphasise her point. Her eyes were wide and shining. 'We have the most advanced musical society in the world here in the GDR, and the state is committed to its support and preservation. We are very lucky, I believe.' I could see Hans nodding more and more emphatically as she went on. 'This is why I play with the band at Café Bruno. Music is not meant to be confined to these few halls. It is something for all times in one's life, for all people. Let them have their *rock and roll'* – she spat the English words – 'our musical life is so much richer here. A richness that could only be achieved through socialism.'

She leant back, satisfied with her lecture. Hans nodded again. He looked impressed.

I wasn't. I was horrified. I had dared to imagine for a moment that Dana was different. That Café Bruno would be a chance to experiment, to explore. I imagined that outside my small and ignorant existence there was a vast world of open-minded musicians waiting to be discovered. I believed it to be my only hope of escape from my adoptive parents' suffocating way of life, the one they wanted me to share. But for Dana, it seemed that music was just another tool for the socialist revolution.

I did not want to join her band.

I spoke. 'Actually, Dana, I have been thinking that

perhaps the commitment required for your band would be a bit too much. These two years before graduation are the most important and I would not want my schoolwork to suffer.'

They both turned to look at me. Hans narrowed his eyes.

'I ... I think the opposite, in fact, Jakob. I think Miss Decker's proposition for you to join her band is a good one. And I agree wholeheartedly with her. We should have different ways of playing and enjoying music, away from the ... the *stuffiness* of the concert hall.' I tried to imagine Hans in some bohemian bar like from a film, knocking back a schnapps and clicking his fingers to jazz. It was sad, rather than amusing. 'I'm sure Miss Decker will take you under her wing. And besides, your schoolwork has already improved a lot – your hard work has paid off.'

What could I do? Defy Hans to his face, in front of Dana?

Dana's eyes glinted in triumph.

'Fantastic. Jakob, I can collect you on the way to your audition. Say, ten o'clock, Sunday morning? I forgot to mention, Mr Eberhardt. Jakob will have to pass an audition before he is allowed to join the band. I'm sure you can understand why.'

Hans and I walked home from the Funkhaus that night.

We were friendly for once and chatted as we walked.

'I can see why you like her,' he told me. 'She is strong-willed, passionate.'

Though I was annoyed about what had happened, I also knew that if Hans was encouraging my musical pursuits then this could be an opportunity. Even if it involved joining some wet Communist idea of a jazz band. I felt a strange sense of hope, for the first time in a long time.

My violin strap shifted on my shoulder and I stopped for a moment to adjust it. Hans walked a few paces ahead.

As I fiddled with the strap, a bright colour caught my eye. There was some kind of note attached to scraps of blue rubber lying next to the hedge we had just passed. Curiosity got the better of me and I quickly bent over to unstick two damp postcards from the shredded balloon. The front of both had the same colour photograph of a sunny day and a garish slogan encouraging the reader to visit West Berlin. I glanced up at Hans and then shoved both cards into my back pocket and walked on.

Alone in my room, I tried to figure out how it could be a trick. Could Hans somehow have dropped the cards for me to find as some kind of test? But then how could he have known I would stop at that exact moment to adjust my strap? And if it wasn't Hans, could it really be someone reaching out from West Berlin? Even if it wasn't someone trying to trick me specifically, that didn't mean it wasn't a trap. The Stasi could be dropping notes like these all over in order to catch potential traitors who wrote back to the address provided.

I knew I would probably never see the light of day again if I was caught, but I had to risk it. I could feel my heart racing, this could be my opportunity to connect with my real mother again. Sometimes, I daydreamed about seeing her and my sister again, but this was the first time I'd ever had a way of possibly contacting her. I knew it was incredibly unlikely to work, but I had to find a way to get a message back to the West undetected. Or, at least, I had to try.

HARRY

I felt more lost than ever after watching my balloon get shot down. I had known it was unlikely to work, but that afternoon had been one of hope for me. In reaching out to someone in the East, I think I was trying to make sense of my life here in Berlin and of what I'd seen. But it had come to nothing. The East German guards had seen to that – or so I thought.

But, a week to the day after I'd watched my message of hope fall from the sky, I unexpectedly found my self-addressed postcard in our mailbox in the lobby. Hastily, I stuffed it into my pocket before taking the rest of the mail up and leaving it on the kitchen table. I had no idea how my parents would react to what I had done, but I suspected that my father wouldn't be happy with me getting involved with something so dangerous.

Back in the safety of my room, I sat at my desk and stared at the postcard. It was bizarre. Although a bit worse for wear from its travels, the card in my hand was definitely the one I had sent over the Wall. Our address was there, written in my own handwriting. But the rest of the postcard was entirely blank.

I sat puzzling over this for a long time, not even getting up to tune my radio to one of the pop stations, which was what I usually did after school. Why would someone send back the postcard blank? Was it a warning? Or a threat, maybe? If so, what was it supposed to mean?

Something else slowly dawned on me. I had smelt a faint scent of lemon ever since arriving home. I had assumed it was something they used to clean the communal areas of our building, but that smell had followed me back to our apartment and into my room. I gave the card a sniff. What was going on? Who had sent me a blank postcard that smelt of lemons? Frustrated, and a little scared, I tore the postcard into several pieces and stuffed it into my desk drawer.

The smell of lemons lingered throughout the evening and found its way into my dreams. The mysterious postcard was my first thought when I woke up in the middle of the night. Hadn't I read something about lemons in one of my comic books? I turned on my bedside lamp and reached for my issue of *The Fly*. I flicked past the life of Jan Jäger to find the page I wanted. There it was – the letter he had written to an accomplice; correspondence travelling from the East into the West. The first panel showed a building, an ugly block of brick. The next showed us inside a mail room where Stasi officers steamed open letters. They were reading the contents before deciding whether or not to let them carry on with their journey through the mail.

They came across The Fly's letter and opened the envelope to reveal blank pages inside. The officers laughed.

Someone has posted a letter but forgotten to write it!
Some people are idiots.

The letter was put back in the envelope and resealed. Then it was placed on the pile deemed non-threatening and allowed to pass without further scrutiny.

The next panel showed The Fly smiling. He knew he would outwit the guards. He had made a solution with water and lemon juice and dipped an inkless fountain pen into it to write his message to the West. The next panel showed a US soldier, The Fly's closest accomplice, receiving the letter in the American Sector. He gently heated it underneath so the words could reveal themselves.

I heard Dieter's voice. 'This is art imitating life.'

I carefully retrieved all the pieces from the drawer and

laid them out next to my lamp. Then I held the first piece over the heat.

I held it there for what seemed like eternity. I felt a bit foolish at first, half-believing it was make-believe and ready to give up. But then I saw the first word appear, the brown letters coming through in English.

help

Then the next words emerged:

Please help find

I grabbed another piece and repeated the process, my fingertips getting burnt in the heat of the lamp. Finally, I pieced this little jigsaw back together to reveal the full message:

Please help find Mother. Frau Ebba Fiedler. She is in the West. I am stuck in the East with no way of reaching her. Your friend, Jakob Fiedler, age 14.

And a return address:

39 Liepnitzstraße, 1031, East Berlin

A shiver went down my spine. I couldn't believe this was happening. It felt like I finally had a reason for being here in Berlin. I moved to the window, pulled back my curtain and looked out into the East. I felt like The Fly in real life. I was now a part of something, not alone any more. Someone needed me, maybe even someone I might one day call a friend.

The next day, I took the postcard to the only person I thought would understand. Dieter.

'I won't waste time lecturing you,' he said, although his slight smile suggested that he was secretly impressed. 'I'm sure you know how silly this was. We maybe don't have to worry about the Stasi on this side of the Wall, but your father is a diplomat, no? Something like this would certainly make things very awkward. And for this Jakob boy, well, it would be much worse for him if this was discovered.'

'Yes, I know, but I'm beginning to think it was worth it.'

Dieter opened the till and took out some notes, pushing them into my hand. 'I have some friends that might be able to help,' he said, 'but in the meantime, take this.'

'I don't need money,' I said, trying to give it back.

'Just take it,' he said. 'Use it to put a message in the newspaper. You never know, she could still be here in Berlin. I would say she is. If her son is trapped over there, I am guessing the mother would not have gone too far. With some luck, someone will see it and pass on your message to her.'

I wondered about Frau Fiedler. I tried to conjure up a picture of what she might look like. I saw a quiet woman with glasses and her hair tied back. I saw a small apartment and a kitchen fitted with modest things, no room for luxury, just a candle lit for her son. Waiting for the day she finds him so that her life could start again.

Thinking about Frau Fiedler reminded me of Mom. How lonely she must be here in Berlin. Her relationship with my father was worse than ever, and while she had done her best to make me feel like I had a home here, what had I done for her?

When I said goodbye to Dieter, I hurried home to see if she was okay.

I headed straight to the stereo when I got in and put on a record that we had brought from home. She followed me into the living room and leant on the doorframe, listening to her favourite album.

'I've not heard this one in a while,' she said. '1956. What a year. You were three years old and it was like the world burst right into colour. All of a sudden there were these "teenagers" everywhere. They were a new thing and I was a bit jealous not to be that young any more. But I had you and your father, so I was happy. Not that that meant I couldn't enjoy a bit of Elvis, though! You know,

I used to sing 'Love Me Tender' to you every night to get you off to sleep.'

I tried to imagine what she would have been like back then.

'How about this one then, Mom?'

I took off Elvis and put on one of the records Dieter had lent me.

'What in the world is this?' she said.

'It's The Rolling Stones,' I said, turning it up loud before reaching out and grabbing her hand and spinning her around, moving with the beat.

'Harry, what are you doing?' she said, laughing.

'There's a revolution going on, Mom, and maybe I want to be a part of it. The young are taking over.'

I spun her outwards and then reeled her back in and she laughed even more.

The music was so loud we didn't hear the door slam or my dad's heavy footsteps. He came storming into the room with a face like thunder.

'What the hell is this?' he said.

'Walt, this is what the kids are listening to,' said my mom, still laughing, still moving with the music, almost breathless from our burst of excitement.

'Music by beatniks and hippies. We're fighting the fight

here in Berlin. There's a war on in Vietnam. And all these idiots can sing about is peace and love. Don't they know it's their freedom we're fighting for?'

He pushed past me and grabbed at the needle on the stereo, scraping it across the vinyl to stop the music.

'What are you doing? You'll scratch it,' I said. I rushed to the stereo, trying to get around him, pulling at his arm, trying to protect the record that Dieter had trusted me with.

My dad spun round. He had the record in his hand.

'Where did you get this from? What else have you been hiding from me?'

Before I could respond, he turned and he threw it against the wall. Mom gasped. I couldn't believe it, either. Dad had always had a bit of a temper, but this was something else. As he turned back to me, he reminded me of a panel in *The Fly*. I saw a black-and-white image of a large East German agent who had The Fly cornered, anger in his eyes.

'You're no better than the Stasi!' I shouted.

I knew it was a mistake, even as the words left my mouth. A look of cold fury came over him then, that I'd never seen before. He came towards me and grabbed me by the shirt collar. Lost for words, he grunted, bared his teeth, inhaled.

My mom came to my aid, screaming, 'Walt, leave him alone!' He let go of me to bat her away and she fell sprawling to the floor with a thud.

She looked up in disbelief. My dad snapped to and said, 'Nancy, I'm so sorry.'

He moved to go and help her up, but she backed away.

'Don't touch me,' she said. But it wasn't fear in her eyes; in that moment she looked as if she hated him.

She got up and left the room without another word. I heard the bedroom door slam.

Dad's shoulders slumped, he looked back at me almost apologetically.

'I didn't mean ...' But then he trailed off.

I picked up the hurled record to check for damage, but I couldn't see clearly. There were tears in my eyes. I could feel my heart pounding. For the first time, I felt that I had no respect for my dad at all.

I missed him. My dad. The one we seemed to have left behind in D.C.

I'm not saying our relationship was perfect back then. But I remembered summer nights throwing a football in the park as the sun went down. Staying just that little bit longer than everyone else.

·I missed that man who could always make Mom and me laugh. Who, ultimately, always had my back.

It seemed like he was a different man entirely to the one I found sitting on my bed when I got home from school that Monday.

My bedroom looked like it had been burgled, my drawers emptied out, my possessions strewn across the floor. Dad was leafing through my copy of *The Fly*. He looked up as I entered; I couldn't meet his eye.

'Where did you get this from?' he said.

'Why, are you going to throw that against the wall too?'

'Seriously, Harry, what is this nonsense? This isn't available from the stores around here, even I know that. Where did you get it from?'

'Nowhere.'

'I'm guessing it was the same place you got those damn records.'

'Yes, fine. I went to a store and bought some records and comic books. What the hell else am I supposed to do in this stupid city?'

He stopped on a page – The Fly with an East German woman, a beautiful blonde he was enticing to gain information.

'Listen to me, Harry, don't mess around. It would be

very bad if you were caught with this kind of stuff. Do you understand the position that would put me in? Have you no respect for the work I am trying to do?'

'Have you even read it?' I asked. 'He's on our side! He's helping people escape from the East to freedom.'

'That's not the point.' Dad sounded like he was trying to stop himself from getting cross again. 'This is contraband, it has been smuggled in from the East. It is absolutely not the kind of thing the son of an American diplomat should be hiding under his mattress.'

He rolled up the comic and put it into his back pocket.

'Harry, I want you to show me the store where you got this from.'

'Why? What are you going to do?'

'Just get in the car. Tell me where it is.'

Dad drove us in silence. It still didn't make sense to me that he would be this bothered about some underground comic book. Sure, The Fly sometimes had to go behind the backs of the authorities in the West to help the people in the East, but at the end of the day he believed in the same thing as my father. Freedom.

We pulled up at a stop light and I thought about just opening my door, throwing myself out and making a run for it. But this was my dad, right? What harm could he do? He was just looking out for me; he probably just wanted to check Dieter out for himself. When he met Dieter, he'd soon realise this wasn't dangerous. We'd be able to talk him round. I'd reassure him there was nothing going on, that I was just into some new stuff, some new music, a new comic to read and what was the big deal?

We pulled up outside Dieter's.

'That's it?' he asked.

'That's it.'

'Come on, come with me.'

Inside, Dad didn't notice the row after row of brightly coloured comic books sitting in the racks.

'Ah, Harry, so good to see you. And I see you've brought a friend with you.'

'I am his father. I am here to tell you to stay away from my son.'

'Dad, what? You can't do that.'

'Quiet, Harry,' said my dad and he yanked at my arm to force his instruction home.

'Sir,' said Dieter, coming from behind the counter, 'I think there must have been a misunderstanding.'

My dad grabbed Dieter's collar just like he had my own.

'No misunderstanding,' he said. 'I don't know where

you get this trash, but it shouldn't be on sale in a store like this and it certainly shouldn't have made its way into my son's possession.'

Dieter hadn't flinched. He had barely even blinked. He stayed calm and matched my dad stare for stare.

He said, 'I can assure you, sir, all I was doing was helping Harry channel the interests he had already shown. He is a fine young man. You must be very proud.'

My dad lowered his tone to a growl.

'Stay away from my son,' he said. 'If you don't, your life can be made very difficult indeed.'

Dieter caught my eye as we left and nodded as if to say, *don't worry, everything will be all right.*

I didn't have time to say goodbye. Dad was already pushing me out the door and bundling me back into the car.

When we got home, the first thing he did was take my copy of *The Fly* and burn it in the kitchen sink. I begged for him to reconsider, tried to explain again that we were on the same side. The Fly was working with the Americans, he was one of us, there were many people in the East that wanted freedom too. I shouted at him to stop, but it was already too late.

The next day, I went out and put the ad in the paper, as Dieter had suggested.

For Frau Ebba Fiedler. I have information on your son, Jakob. Please contact H.R.

JAKOB

Café Bruno is on a corner of Friedrichstraße, a curving, cobbled avenue whose western side is the first frontier of the Wall. There is a row of huge white wooden panels topped with barbed wire and blocking the view of No Man's Land. The café has frosted glass windows; the lettering above the front door is missing the 'R'. Inside, the main room is lined with black leather banquettes. There is a bar of reddish wood that always holds a couple of cake stands, and a raised stage in the back corner. Behind the bar there always hangs a blackboard with the specials.

Dana had picked me up from the Eberhardts' apartment at ten o'clock exactly. When the electric bell rang, I made to run down with my violin, but Hans stopped me and insisted Dana come up. He greeted her with a firm handshake and a friendly pat on the shoulder. He offered her coffee, but she told him in her professional, polite way that she could not accept, as it would make us late for my audition.

On the walk there, half an hour or so through the empty Sunday morning streets, there was no conversation. I was preoccupied, wondering how I could intentionally fail this audition, and though Dana glanced my way once or twice, she said nothing. I was grateful for this. She seemed like the kind of ambitious young socialist who would prattle on about the party and my brilliant adopted father, and while I had to keep up appearances for the duration of the audition, I wasn't sure how far my patience would stretch if she started spouting the usual politics. Some part of me had wanted to believe that she might be something special, someone to show me another world. But her behaviour towards Hans made that seem hopeless.

Dana's band were called The Stamp Collectors. They were tuning up when we reached the café. Dana made the introductions. There was mustachioed Ralf on drums; Nadine, running through rapid scales on the piano; lanky Cristopher on accordion and, finally, Viktor on trombone. They glanced at me without smiling when Dana told them my name.

'No singer?' I asked.

'Not normally,' replied Viktor. 'Occasionally one of our friends ...' He was the oldest of the group. About twenty, I guessed. The rest were closer to Dana's age, although I was clearly the youngest.

I unpacked my violin and we began to play. The first piece of music lined up for my audition was a song about a Brazilian woman walking through the streets of Rio de Janeiro. I had planned a strategy: I was going to play well but slip in a few offensive mistakes. I reasoned that to do more than that would be too obvious.

But 'The Girl from Ipanema' was a song I knew well from Western radio, and it was a song I loved. From the first bar, I knew I couldn't play it badly. Or not intentionally, anyway. Somehow I managed to mess up the beginning to the first chorus, but nobody batted an eyelid – Ralf just kept tapping away steadily and the song danced on. After that, we played several other jazz classics I knew from the radio but would never have played at school, or in the orchestra at the Funkhaus. Anywhere, in fact, except for my room, when no one else was listening. And everything about the playing was different. The band interacted with each other – glances and nods as the tempo sped up or slowed down, or looks of cautious anticipation when the music approached the more dramatic sections. At one point, Dana gave me a lop-sided smile when I improvised over the main melody Nadine was picking out on the piano.

And they were good – very good. Dana, I had seen before, but her playing here was different – less controlled, funkier. Cristopher's accordion sighed quietly, then burst into brilliant solos. Nadine's fingers blurred across the keyboard, making it sing. Viktor was a steady, tuneful trombonist, never making a mistake. Ralf seemed to have an eye on everyone, guiding the rest of the musicians back to the group if they went too far astray.

I became so engrossed that I forgot about my plan to botch the audition.

I forgot it was an audition.

After forty minutes, Cristopher said, 'Coffee?' and everyone agreed. It transpired that he worked a few shifts at the café, and he busied himself behind the bar, returning with a silver pot on a tray. We all sat at a table near the stage.

'Nice fiddle-playing,' said Nadine and, to my surprise, everyone agreed. I felt intimidated by such talented musicians. I could not believe they would regard me as an equal. 'Where did you learn?'

'My mother taught me,' I said, and then panicked because it was generally safer not to mention my birth parents. 'I mean, not Margot, obviously. I guess I mostly learnt at school.'

Dana spoke next, as if to save me from my embarrassment. 'Well, Jakob, what do you think about our little band here, then? You seemed into it. Not too bad, yes?'

'Better than that,' I said, quietly. I could feel my face getting hot.

'So,' she continued, 'normally we gig about once every month, rehearse here Sunday mornings, sometimes Saturdays too. We get paid a few marks, but, most importantly, you can eat as many of Gerold's cakes as you want.' The band chuckled at this. Ralf puffed his cheeks out and rubbed a hand on his stomach. 'We just played a gig on Friday. How do you feel about coming to a few practices, and, if it works out, playing at our next show?'

I wondered then, about this group, what they really wanted from me. I had enjoyed playing the music, it was true, but I was a citizen of the GDR, and I knew first-hand how my country worked. I was a route to Hans, presumably. But for what purpose? Did Dana want a favourable word for when she applied for postings to teach music? Did the band think I could help them get approved for radio play by the Culture department?

Or perhaps, a voice inside of me piped up, *they are musicians like me, who just want to make something beautiful.*

Perhaps Dana had approached me because she genuinely thought I was good.

It didn't matter. I didn't care about politics. All I knew, all I understood, was that this was another opportunity to play music. Real music with real musicians. Music that was alive.

I joined The Stamp Collectors.

Hans, of course, was delighted. 'You have impressed me, Jakob. I look forward to hearing everything about your new role. Everything, yes? We will come and see you play some time, won't we, Margot?'

Margot squeezed my upper arm, crinkled her eyes. 'Oh, we're so very proud of you, Jakob.'

The following evening, another postcard arrived.

Luckily, one of my chores was to collect the mail from the rows of metal boxes in the foyer of our apartment block, so it was me that found the small rectangular card sat between two unassuming envelopes addressed to Hans. My heart skipped a beat when I saw my name and address carefully written on the reverse. I shoved it inside my jacket and made myself look around, to check that no one was watching from the shadows of the empty entrance hall.

I had not dared to hope for a reply. I raced upstairs and hid the card in my underwear drawer. I didn't take it out again to look at it until at least an hour after Hans and Margot had gone to sleep.

On the front, a slogan offered me 'Greetings from Berlin!' The background was a series of small, square pictures from the West – gleaming cars filing past shopping centres, glittering city squares at night. On the back, a message written in English:

Dear Jakob,

Wish you were here!

Your true friend,

Harry

But I had known from the moment I'd found the postcard, from the scent of lemons, that there was another, hidden message. I was excited that Harry must have figured out the trick I had learnt at school – how to use lemon juice as invisible ink. With a box of matches I'd nabbed from the kitchen, I set to revealing it. Between the lines were other lines, written in tiny crabbed characters revealed in the heat from the flame. They appeared faint brown on the off-white of the card. Unfortunately, they were written in English, and English was one of the subjects I most relied on Jürgen for help with. But I had my textbook, and, slowly, I translated it.

Dear Jakob,
Thank you for your message. I am glad to have found a friend across the Wall.

Wish you were here!
I am looking for your mother and will write as soon as I have more information.

Your true friend,
and ally in the fight for democracy and freedom.

Harry Rogers
PS Please write and let me know this reached you. Tell me about yourself, about life in the East.

Once I was sure I had captured the full meaning of the postcard, I burnt it and tossed the ashes from my window. I watched them flutter and twist in the orange glow from the street lamps. They fell to the ground like black snowflakes. It was two in the morning. I went to sleep and did not dream of anything.

Margot's hand on my shoulder woke me, and at first I panicked, casting my eye about the room for any incriminating evidence. But I had hidden the box of matches under the bed and replaced the textbook on its shelf.

'Are you OK?' she said, looking at me with her pale eyes. I nodded mutely. 'You must have slept through your alarm. You'll be late. I brought you this.' She left a plate with a slice of toasted and buttered rye bread on the side.

The full weight of what the postcard meant struck me, lying there in bed. Not the fact that it was against the rules to receive such a postcard, though I was well aware of that. But here, for the first time, was a lifeline, however slight it might be. Harry Rogers, whoever he was, and whatever his motives were, was looking for my mother in West Berlin. I felt a small pang of guilt, for Harry talked about 'democracy' and 'freedom', but those things meant very little to me. All I cared about was the small possibility that he might be able to reach my family.

And then what? Would my family be able to arrange for me to join them across the Wall? That was too much to hope for, surely. Even a letter, just to know they were alive, would be a miracle. The postcard was a ray of hope from another world.

In the space of two days, my life had changed, unfolded in ways I could not have predicted. Before, the future had seemed grey, grim, concrete. Now the future was unknowable, as if I was pushing through endless dark curtains, unsure where I would emerge. Unsafe, perhaps, but there was a chance of something good happening – even if it was just a small chance …

I wrote back to Harry that very morning. During school break, I locked myself in a toilet cubicle. I had two pens – one to write in ink, the other spilling drops from my bottle of lemon juice. I ran out of school to post my reply, so I was ten minutes late to physics and the teacher scratched a black mark in her register.

Dear Harry,

I'm so grateful to you for helping me. I miss my mother terribly and pray that she's alive.

Life here is good.

I don't know what to tell you about the East. It's where I've always lived.

I play violin and I have just joined a band that I am very excited about.

It's all I know. There are many good people here. But many people who are driven to do bad things. For me, it is like a shadow over everything.

Do you like music?

It was my mother who taught me how to play. Music is like a link to her and my previous life.

I also play in an orchestra at the Funkhaus, perhaps you have heard of it?

It has been years since I've spoken with my real family. Please do everything you can to find my mother and my sister, Katrin.

Do write back and tell me about your life.

I would love to hear about the West, we never know what to believe here. Do you really have a hundred kinds of chocolate bar to choose from in your stores?

I hope we will become good friends.

Jakob

And so our secret correspondence began. With so much to say, we moved from postcards to letters, which we exchanged at the rate of one a week or so. What with them and the band, I actually found myself feeling hopeful, and even happy. But I was also paranoid that our simple solution for hiding our words would not fool the people checking the mail. I knew word would quickly get back to Hans if we were discovered. So I became more adept at hiding the scent of lemons. I started hanging my letters out in my room for an hour or two to let it dissipate while I practised the songs for The Stamp Collectors. Somehow, there was always a slight smell left behind.

Harry and I, in the visible content of our letters, pretended to be innocent pen-pals.

'What music are you listening to?'

'How's school going?'

'Hasn't the weather been nice recently?'

But behind that, I used the hidden words to tell him

about my family. My real family. And about my mother especially. I tried to paint a portrait of her, as if that would help him with his search. I told him about my early memories of her cooking and laughing and playing violin. How she always seemed to be smiling and could make other people smile too. How safe she made me feel and how much I missed her. I tried to give him a physical description of her, in case that was of some use in the search. I knew she had brown hair and blue eyes and I remembered her as being tall – but was that because I was smaller then? I didn't even have a photograph of her, so I didn't know whether to trust the image in my memory. And I had no way of knowing how much she would have changed over the years.

Over the next few weeks, I found that the correspondence we wrote to fool the guards became almost as important to me as the hidden updates. I was amazed to discover that Harry was almost the same age as me, that our interests were similar. He read the listings for radio shows broadcast from the American Sector and recommended certain programmes I should listen to (these parts were written in lemon juice in case they were seen as unpatriotic). I imagined him lying in his bed on the other side of the Wall, listening to the same scratchy guitars, the same energetic frontmen shouting about revolution. I had never liked rock and roll before. I thought it was loud and a bit childish. But then I heard, on Harry's recommendation, a guy called Bob Dylan and before long I was listening to all kinds of new bands.

I told no one about Harry. I knew it was a risk to reach out to him, but it had felt like fate finding that postcard, and I had to believe he was for real. I tried not to think about what Hans would do if he ever found out. Or worse still, what one of his rivals might do if they discovered the son of a high-ranking Stasi official was writing to a 'chewing-gum eater', as they used to call Americans during the war. Everyone whispered at school about what happened to traitors. There were large prison camps in Russia, full of such people, left to be forgotten about, out of public view. If you were questioned by the Stasi, though, there was no guarantee you would even make it that far. I knew from Hans' skirting of the subject that my school friends were not too far from the mark.

Whenever a letter arrived from Harry, after I had applied the candle flame, I scanned it first for mention of my mother. But he didn't seem to be making any progress. In those weeks, I fantasised that Harry had heard from her, that he had met her, but he was keeping it a surprise until he could manage to put us in touch. The next letter would contain faked papers that I could use to cross the Wall and join them. But that was too much like a story from one of the comic books Harry told me about. I soon learnt to stop myself going into the fantasy.

Music kept me going. At the Funkhaus, I spent my time in the recording studios during sessions with the orchestras. I would man the desk when the recording engineers took a break to smoke. People began to mention opportunities for me, things I might consider applying for in my final year of school – always, it seemed to me, with the unwelcome hint that my family connections might make the application process a little smoother. I continued to play in the orchestra there, but The Stamp Collectors had become my real musical outlet.

I met Gerold Klug, the manager of Café Bruno. Dana introduced me one afternoon before the café opened. Gerold was arranging a row of enormous chocolate éclairs in a fan shape on a glass plate, his fingers delicately equalising the angles between them. He didn't notice me at first, and then looked up in surprise, his mouth in an 'O' that broke into a huge grin.

'So, you're Jakob Eberhardt. They tell me you can play. Thank goodness! Someone in that band needs to ...'

He was a big man, tall and fat, his round face red from the heat of the café. Dana and the others joked about his cakes and his size. He never seemed to mind. He laughed it off with a huge roar, hands balled into fists on his hips, rocking backwards and forwards at the waist.

My first gig with The Stamp Collectors was booked on the evening that I received my fifth letter from Harry. I felt sure as I picked the letter up from the mailbox that this would be the letter where Harry told me he had found my mother. But the letter was taken up with chat about music, comic books, and a film he had been to see, and then, revealed by the flame of the candle: Ebba: no news. I felt a wave of frustration. I liked Harry. I liked what I knew about him. But I did not want a friend. I wanted my family back.

I was the last to arrive at Café Bruno, and though I was only five minutes late, Dana gave me a short look.

'We've already handed out set lists. What's that?'

I had been reading Harry's letter again as I was walking to the café, hoping against hope that I had missed something in the translation. Now I shoved it in the back pocket of my trousers.

'Nothing,' I said, 'Just a letter.'

Dana paused for a moment between adjusting the tuning knobs on her double bass. I felt the need to break the silence. 'It's from my girlfriend,' I said, absurdly.

Dana's smirk was back. 'A girlfriend, eh? You didn't mention this before.'

'Yes, yes, um – she lives in Leipzig. We met on a cultural exchange.'

'I see, well, I'm very happy for you both, but please don't let it distract you from your playing.'

We were due on at eight.

Hans was unable to attend due to work commitments, and I knew that Margot would not come without him. *But I look forward to hearing how it went, how everyone was, when you get back in*, Hans had said.

Margot had looked at her watch. I'd noticed that her hand trembled. 'You'll be back by ten forty-five, yes?'

There was an odd, nervous atmosphere in the band that night. Viktor drummed his fingers on his music stand constantly, scanning the room. Cristopher seemed on edge, pacing up and down on the hardwood floor in front of the stage. I assumed it was because it was their first gig with me, and I resolved to focus my concentration as well I could.

Then, before I knew it, we were playing. A decent-sized crowd had turned up to see us – thirty or forty people standing around the room, watching as we started to play. There was a desperate energy to our music that night. Ralf hit the snares and cymbals with force, and the rest of the band responded in kind, playing louder and more aggressively than we had during practice. We played fast, and the crowd's applause grew louder. But to me, it felt as if something was off – the rest of the band seemed awkward, stiff. At one point, Dana hit the wrong string, and the bad note rang false across the room. I glanced over at her and smiled. When she made mistakes like this during practice – and she didn't make many – she usually just gave a shrug. But this time I could not catch her eye. Her face was unsmiling, staring out into the audience.

As suddenly as it had begun, the gig ended, and applause washed over us. Gerold appeared with a tray of Vita Colas and he went around the group, handing them out. 'Great show, great show,' he said.

'Did everything go all right?' asked Cristopher.

Gerold wouldn't know, I thought. I had noticed that the manager had ducked out a couple of times to the back room, so he hadn't even seen the whole show.

'Everything went perfectly,' said Gerold. 'Now relax, yes?'

I could not relax. For, though the applause of the audience was flattering, once we stopped playing, I could feel the letter, heavy in my back pocket. How could I take joy in music when my family were out there somewhere, without me?

I took a seat in a banquette by the window in the front, and stared out at the dark, the Wall flattened to a vague white by frosting on the glass. My family might have been no more than a hundred metres away. Yet between me and them was a stretch of concrete and barbed wire and guards and machine-gun posts so impassable it might as well have been an ocean.

Dana came and sat beside me. She was smiling; the tension from the performance had evaporated.

'The show went well, don't you agree? The audience seemed to think so.'

'Sure,' I said. Usually I found her interesting, but right then I wanted to be left alone with my thoughts.

'You were the right choice, you know? We all think so, we knew it as soon as you played with us. We're pleased to have you. You'll stay with us, won't you?'

I turned towards her. She was smiling. I noticed a thick strand of her hair had somehow come apart and stuck out at the side. I wanted to reach up to put it back in place but thought better of it.

Then her smile dimmed. 'You didn't enjoy it?'

'No, no. It's late, that's all.'

'Why so melancholy? Come on, I'll get you another cola.'

I put my hand over my glass. 'No, thank you. I need to head back soon.'

'Ah! I see!' Her eyebrows rose in a teasing way. 'The studious schoolboy. Can't be late. No, not with your parents.'

Perhaps I was tired for, before I knew it, I snarled back at her. 'They are not my parents.'

Dana's head pulled back from mine.

'I'm sorry,' I said. 'I need to go, that's all.' I pushed her away from me and started moving to get out of the banquette. I was ashamed that I had let my emotions get the better of me.

Dana did not stand to let me pass. She spoke quietly. 'I know,' she said. 'I know what they ... what the State did to your family. It's disgusting.'

I blinked at her, shocked. I had never heard anyone criticise the State so openly. I hadn't been crazy to think Dana might be different. Though I knew my adoption by the Eberhardts was common knowledge, no one ever spoke to me about it.

I didn't know what to say. I sank back into my seat, my mind racing. I realised her performance for Hans was an act, just like my own. She reached out and placed her hand on mine, squeezing it for a second.

'Tell me about them,' she said. 'About your real parents.'

And something about the way she looked at me then, the gentle note in her voice, made me want to tell her. And before I knew it, I was opening up about everything. About my parents and Katrin. About our suburban apartment, which in my memory was always filled with honey-coloured sunlight and the sound of my mother's violin. I told her about how we would sing traditional songs as a family. About how my mother would play violin and my father the piano, as well as leading the singing. How he taught Katrin and I the harmonies and never corrected us if we were flat.

Dana listened closely to everything. I went on. I told her about my parents' friends, the late-night meetings that would happen at our apartment, when Katrin and I would be told to go to bed. How my mother would sneak up afterwards to tuck us in, kiss our foreheads goodnight.

And then I told her something I had never told anyone before. About the day when the phone call came. The rush from the apartment. The tiny suitcase I was told to carry. The warm feel of my mother's cheek on mine the last time I saw her. The terrible, terrible wait in that train carriage. The guards bundling my father into the back of a van.

A tear escaped my eye and slid down my cheek.

Dana rested a hand on mine on the table. 'Your parents,'

she said. There was no need for her to clarify which parents she meant. 'What happened to them?'

'My mother and my sister are in the West, I think. I have not heard from them since I was six.'

She shook her head slowly. 'And your father?'

'He died. In prison. I don't know what happened exactly, they wouldn't tell me.'

I remembered the afternoon Hans and Margot had come to me in my bedroom and told me of my father's death. How sad Margot looked, and how she had pressed me to her chest, and told me that if I wanted to cry it was fine, that I should let it all out.

'I'm sorry,' said Dana. 'Who knows what might have happened? We have heard of the State trying to cover up for the police before. Interrogations that get out of hand ...' Her gaze drifted across the café to the now-empty stage.

'But your mother and sister are still alive?' she said, facing me again.

'I think so, yes – they escaped into the West, they must have done.' I thought about telling her about Harry, but I knew it would be dangerous for both of us if I did.

She bit her bottom lip and looked at me closely. 'So, would you like to go to the West?'

I shrugged. Of course I did. But I didn't want to get

carried away with dreams. 'I'm still at school, Dana, and you know who Hans is. I won't get a day pass, not ever. I can't just float through the Wall.'

'Maybe not ... but can you keep a secret? A very important secret?' I nodded. 'Then follow me.'

She stood up and took my hand, leading me towards the bar. As she approached, Gerold looked up from pouring out a glass of schnapps. He looked from Dana to me, then back to Dana. Something passed between them.

Dana pushed open the door behind the bar. We went through to the kitchen in the back, where normally Gerold prepared the plates of pastries. Gerold followed behind us. His meaty hand squeezed my shoulder.

'I think you're right about this one, Dana,' he said, looking into my eyes. 'And Gerold's intuition isn't often wrong.'

Dana fumbled with a drawer full of documents, and then she rolled out a large piece of paper on the big kitchen table. She beckoned us over. A map of Berlin, East and West. The Wall was a thick red line snaking through the middle.

And there was another line, a straight black line, much shorter, crossing the red one. It started, I noticed, here on Friedrichstraße.

'What is this?' I asked, staring stupidly at the map.

'We can trust you, right, Jakob? If you let slip to Hans … well, that would be the end for all of us.'

'You don't need to worry about that,' I replied. 'I hate him more than anyone.'

'Good, that's what I thought,' she said, nodding. 'Well, Jakob, we're building a tunnel.'

A tunnel? I couldn't believe it. I looked to Gerold. He pointed downwards.

'To the West,' he said. 'Starting right here, in the basement.'

'Here,' repeated Dana, 'then under the Wall. We're going to escape. We're going to take you with us to West Berlin and we are going to find your family. I swear it.' Her eyes gleamed.

I looked down at the map again. It was then I noticed it. My mouth went dry and sticky.

The black line of the tunnel stretched for about 120 metres from Café Bruno, all the way to Wilhelmstraße in West Berlin.

Wilhelmstraße. That was Harry's address.

'I think I know someone who can help.'

HARRY

I got home from school and found my mom sitting at the kitchen table waiting for me.

'How could you be so stupid?' she said.

She was in her housecoat, hair wild, looking like she'd just got out of bed. Cigarette butts were piled in the ashtray in front of her.

'What are you talking about?'

'This,' she said, and she held up a letter.

'Oh.' My heart dropped. I had been so careful, always making sure to check the post on my way out to school, before Mom was usually even out of bed. But today there hadn't been any post. I was sure of it. Or it must have come late.

'"Oh". Is that all you've got to say? Who is this Jakob? Why is he writing to you from the East?'

'Erm,' my mind was racing, 'he's kind of a pen-friend. It's a thing from school. We all have to write to someone on the other side of the Wall.'

'I don't think so, Harry. Your school would never encourage you to contact *Communists*. And certainly not without your parents' permission. I hardly think your dad would have consented to this. Oh God, what is he going to say?'

'Mom, please don't tell him.'

'I haven't decided what I am going to do yet.'

She went to the window to smoke another cigarette, the smoke coiling out into the afternoon air and drifting towards the East. I could tell by the movement of her shoulders that she was crying again.

She finished her cigarette and turned to me.

'Go to your room. I don't want to see you until dinner.'

I picked up my school bag and heard her turn on the hob behind me.

I walked down the corridor to my bedroom and heard Mom over my shoulder, talking to herself as she set the postcard on fire and dropped it into the sink.

'And why does it smell like lemons?' she muttered to herself.

I hadn't been back to Dieter's store since my dad's visit. I couldn't face it. Couldn't bear that Dieter might think less of me because of my dad. But after my mom's discovery, I was worried about the notes. and about whether she would tell Dad. I realised I was in danger, and I had put my family in danger too. I needed someone to talk to.

When I got to the store, it was closed. Not just closed, boarded up.

There was tape across the front and a sign that stated, 'No Longer Trading'.

I knocked loudly on the door.

'Dieter! Dieter, are you there? It's me, Harry!'

No response.

What had my dad done?

I couldn't just leave. I had to find out what had happened. I made my way to the alley around the back and counted my way along to the back of Dieter's store. The gate to the small yard behind the building was shut, but not locked. I knew The Fly wouldn't give up at this point. He'd keep going until he got to the bottom of things.

As I pushed the gate open, it was immediately obvious that something was wrong – the bins had been knocked over and their contents scattered. The door to the rear of the store was hanging open.

Tentatively, I made my way up the steps. My heart was racing as I pushed the door. Unlocked again. It opened into that familiar back room where Dieter had presented me with a copy of *The Fly*. There was his brown chair and his lamp, his little kitchenette where a pile of washing-up still sat waiting to be done. I'd half-expected the place to have been ransacked, but it seemed almost normal. Everything was just a little out of place, like someone had been through there, but hadn't felt the need to leave a mess.

A floorboard creaked as I made my way slowly down the corridor into the front of the store. Once again, I had the feeling that things were just a little off. The shelves that had held some of the stranger-looking German-language comics had been cleared and some of the other shelves looked more dishevelled than Dieter ever allowed them to get. But in the half of the store where I spent most of my time, the part with the English-language comics and the superheroes, things looked just as they had done the last time I'd been there. One could almost imagine Dieter had just popped out for a minute.

It was only when I made my way back into the little living room that I noticed the most obvious sign that someone other than Dieter had been here. His fake television was still on the little stand opposite his armchair, but the screen had been smashed. How had I not noticed that before? And, of course, his collection of *The Fly* that had once been hidden inside was all gone.

It was my dad's doing, it had to be. Not that he would have been here again himself, but he must have arranged things somehow. He must have used his position to have Dieter removed. I could feel the rage building inside me. I had to confront him.

I arrived home out of breath, my pulse throbbing in my head. My dad was in his study, reading glasses at the end of his nose, top button undone, tie loosened, shirt-sleeves rolled up, and a Bourbon on the desk in front of him. He looked like he hadn't slept much.

He was studying a file when I made my presence known at the door. He didn't look up, didn't take his eyes off the papers he was reading.

'What is it, Harry?'

'The store is closed. Dieter's. But I guess that isn't news to you.'

'I told you to stay away from that store.' He paused, marking something on the page he was reading. 'And I was right to. We ran some checks. It's my job to protect you, to protect West Berlin.'

'What are you talking about?'

'It turns out your friend is dangerous. A troublemaker.

We don't want his kind in the West. I arranged for him to return to the East.'

'You did *what*?'

'He didn't belong here.'

'This is all complete rubbish. I don't believe you.'

I could see his jaw tense. He looked up at me, finally. He put the file on his desk and removed his glasses.

'Don't get involved with the East again,' he said. 'That's part of the reason I burnt your dumb comic. It's not right making entertainment out of something so grave.'

I thought of Dieter being taken by surprise. I imagined a group of masked men rushing in and ordering his hands in the air before cuffing him and removing him entirely from his life.

'People like your friend,' he said, 'they cause trouble. Just look at the protests they had here last year. What do these students have to complain about, anyway? They have a good life here, do you think they would have decided to protest of their own accord? No, it was Commies like your friend whispering in their ears. We can't take risks when it comes to this kind of thing. People like your store owner have to be kept in their place. They need to be contained with the rest of them.'

'Like pigs in a pen?'

'Exactly,' he said, nodding at me, a stiff smile squeezed on to his face. 'Like pigs in a pen.'

I walked away in shock. I couldn't believe what my father had done. Dieter had escaped to the West because he was not safe in the East. But it turned out that people like him, people who questioned what was going on, weren't safe – even in the supposedly free world. Not so long as someone like my father took against them.

The next day, I went out and bought two lemons. I went home and wedged a chair underneath the handle of the door to my room. I was no longer worried that my mom would tell my dad what had happened – she would have kept hold of the evidence if she'd planned on doing that. And after seeing her trying for so long to get my dad to take us back to Washington, I felt as if she was on my side rather than his. But that didn't mean I wouldn't have to be more careful.

I took out my fountain pens and my pot of ink and set them aside. I cut the lemon and squeezed it into a small cup of water and swirled the two together.

Dear Jakob,

Apologies, I was unable to read your latest letter as my mom intercepted it before I had the opportunity.

I hope you are well and enjoying the beautiful weather

we have had the last couple of days.

Please don't worry, I believe we are safe for the time being.
She believes we are just pen-friends, and I don't think she'll
tell my dad.

Did you see the meteor pass over, the night before
last? My grandma always used to tell me
that they granted you a wish.

To avoid detection in the future, I suggest writing to another
address: 17 Solmstraße, 1096, West Berlin.

I hope that yours will come true soon.

Still no news on Ebba, but I will keep searching, we will find her.

All my best,

Harry

The return address I gave him was for Dieter's store. I wasn't at all sure the mailman would deliver to a boarded-up shopfront, but it was too dangerous to keep receiving letters at home.

I stopped by the store the next day after school. Jakob wouldn't have even received my letter yet, let alone replied, but I wanted to make sure the letterbox was at least accessible when the mailman did turn up. I let myself in through the back again, just for a quick look round. A small pile of post had built up by the door and I wondered who might be trying to contact Dieter. I thought about opening it all but felt too guilty. I knew I wouldn't want anyone to read my letters to Jakob. I left them neatly to one side on the till.

I hadn't intended to stay very long, but I found myself wanting to tidy up, to try to make the place look presentable. I wanted the store to feel welcoming if Dieter ever managed to come back. I spent an hour or two straightening up the comic books and other bits and pieces, and even found the old broom to give the floor a sweep.

It was getting dark as I left that evening. I almost walked straight into the tall, middle-aged lady dressed head-to-toe in black who was coming into the yard through the back gate. Startled, I jumped backwards and looked for a route to make a run for it. But there was something about her calm demeanour that made me pause. She didn't seem like the kind of person who was likely to be working for my dad or for the German authorities and I wasn't sure I could get away anyway. Maybe I could trust her.

'*Entschuldigung*,' I said. 'Excuse me.' I was wracking my brain for a way to explain my being there.

'*Hallo*,' she said. '*Wer bist du?*'

'*Ich bin* Harry, Harry Rogers. I'm a friend of Dieter's.'

'A friend of Dieter, eh?' she said, switching to a heavily accented but fluent English. 'Well, any friend of Dieter's is a friend of mine, I'm sure. *Ich bin* Marie. Dieter and I go way back, but I don't think you'll find him here any more.'

'No, I know. And I think it's my fault.'

'Ah, well, that seems unlikely. But why don't you come in with me and tell me about it?'

I probably shouldn't have put my trust in a stranger, but after Dieter's disappearance and with my dad acting so strangely, perhaps I just wanted someone to confide in. It seemed the most natural thing in the world to follow Marie back into Dieter's quiet little room. She moved around as if she knew the place well. My heart rate slowly returned to normal as she put the kettle to boil on the hob and made us both a cup of hot chocolate. It reminded me of the evening I had spent with Dieter when he had told me about the war. There was something reassuring about this woman; she seemed like a connection back to my friend.

We sat and talked a long time that evening. Like Dieter, Marie was from just outside of Berlin originally, but she now lived in the West German capital, Bonn. She came to see her friends in West Berlin every couple of months, which was how she'd heard about Dieter's disappearance. She'd come over that evening to see if she could find any clue to where he might have gone.

'Not that there's much doubt who's taken him,' she said.

I told her about my becoming friends with Dieter.

About my dad discovering my copy of *The Fly* and our visit to the store. I hesitated before telling her that it was him who had had Dieter sent away.

'That's strange,' she said. 'It wouldn't be sanctioned by anyone here in the West. Be very careful, Harry.'

I wasn't sure if I should tell her about Jakob. The last thing I wanted to do was to put him in any danger. But then I remembered that question he always asked in his letters. The promise I'd made him to find his mother. And as Marie was a friend of Dieter's, I thought maybe she'd be able to help. The ad in the newspaper hadn't resulted in any leads, so I needed to try other ways of finding Frau Fiedler.

'Yes,' she said, 'of course I'll ask around. I have many friends who used to live in the East. Someone will know someone – that is always how these things work. Don't worry, Harry, we will find her.'

We decided we would meet back at the store again in exactly two months, when she was due to visit Berlin again. If either of us was unable to attend for any reason on the day, we agreed to leave a short note for the other under the corner of the till, written in lemon juice.

As we were leaving, she took my hands in hers. 'We'll find your friend's mother,' she told me. 'I know it is something Dieter would have cared about. I'm so glad we bumped into each other.'

'I'm glad too,' I said.

'*Auf Wiedersehen.*'

'Goodbye.'

I went back to the store again after school the next afternoon, and again the day after that. I hated spending time at home, hated seeing my dad at all, so I was grateful to have somewhere else to hang out. And being there felt like it brought me closer to Dieter.

Returning on Saturday morning, I saw an envelope lying just inside the door. I recognised Jakob's handwriting on the front immediately.

Dear Harry,

I was so glad to receive your latest letter.

Are you sure we are safe now that your mother knows?
Perhaps it would be better to write less often.

Thank you for recommending some of your favourite bands, I didn't expect to enjoy some of your suggestions as much as I have.

The letter your mother intercepted contained important news from me.
We have a plan to escape the East.

I've even introduced my friend Dana, from The Stamp Collectors, to a couple of the artists you suggested. We may try and cover a couple of songs at our next gig.

We are building a tunnel. It will extend from Café Bruno, under the Wall.

Have you managed to find any recordings of Bach's sonatas yet? I know you aren't the biggest fan of classical music, but I'm sure you would enjoy them if you gave them a chance.

The reason I am risking telling you about this is that the tunnel will surface somewhere near Wilhelmstraße.

Especially, his first sonata, which means a great deal to me.

We need you, Harry. You are the only person we can trust to find somewhere safe for us to break through into the West. Do you know of anywhere, can you find a place?

Yours in anticipation,
Jakob

PS Any news on my mother?

I gasped to myself in Dieter's empty store. I couldn't believe it. I could not believe that they were trying something so crazy. It was horrifying. It was ridiculously stupid. It was fantastic.

I'd heard about different attempts to escape from the East in real life, as well as in *The Fly*. There was the couple who had escaped across the River Spree, pushing their three-year-old daughter in a bathtub. And the delivery man who had smashed through the Wall with his van. But the tunnels were perhaps the most impressive. Digging a tunnel took a lot of planning and effort, but could mean getting dozens of people out, all at once. The kids at school still talked about Tunnel 57, a successful attempt from a couple of years ago. It was named after the number of people who had escaped through it into the basement of an empty bakery. But I had only ever heard of tunnels like that being dug by people in the West who wanted to help people in the East. It was obviously safer that way, with the entrance away from the spying eyes of the Stasi. And even then, many more attempts failed than succeeded, with the collaborators usually ending up in prison, or worse.

I tore up the letter after reading it, as I always did, and headed straight back to Wilhelmstraße, leaving the tattered bits in trash cans along the way. If Jakob was set on this plan, I had to find him a suitable location for the tunnel to surface. Finally, I could do something useful for my friend. I had a new mission.

JAKOB

It wasn't until the following week that I finally got to see the tunnel. I'd wanted to grab a spade and join the diggers immediately when I found out about it, of course, but Gerold had put his foot down on that one.

'It is too much of a risk,' he'd said. 'It is better that you don't meet the people down there now. If you don't know them, you cannot be forced to give them up.'

I'd thought about how I'd suggested to Hans that I could listen out for dangerous talk and realised how much trust Dana and Gerold were putting in the adopted son of a Stasi official.

They were sitting waiting for me when I arrived at the café that Wednesday.

'We have finished early today,' said Gerold, and his glance downwards was enough to tell me what he meant. *Too many 'good citizens' hanging around.*

'There's been a lot of Stasi activity in the area,'

Dana confirmed, 'so Gerold sent the boys home for the afternoon. But the good news is, that means you can see the tunnel. We'll take you down after practice.'

The two hours of practice felt very long. Finally, Gerold led the way down the steep steps into the basement. I had played terribly throughout our practice session. I was too excited about seeing the tunnel to care about making simple mistakes on songs I already knew.

I felt the hairs on the back of my neck prickle and the temperature seemed to drop a couple of degrees as we entered a narrow, low-ceilinged corridor with storage rooms either side. The walls closed in a little and the dust in the air caught in my throat, making me cough. Dana and Gerold led me to the furthest room and I had to duck slightly to fit through the low wooden door. I could feel my heart rate rising – a combination of excitement at seeing the tunnel and nervousness at being in such a confined space. Gerold bent down to plug something in and suddenly, a surprisingly large room was lit up by a series of electric lamps around the walls.

I had imagined the tunnel would start as a hole in the wall, perhaps with a barrel rolled across to hide it when not in use. Instead, I was surprised to see a huge hole dug into the floor by the back wall. It must have been two metres across and at least twice that in depth. Big enough to fit two of Gerold, one on top of the other.

'The water pipes,' Gerold explained, 'and the sewage lines. We have to go deep enough that we don't disturb them. Plus, while I don't think many of us have tried digging from East to West, there have been plenty of attempts to come the other way. The *Vopo* know what to listen for, so the deeper we go, the less chance of detection.'

Dana stamped her foot against the concrete floor.

'This is what they were doing the other night,' she said. 'Most of the digging can be done with regular trowels and spades, but we had to get picks to break through the surface. The noise, you know ...'

So that was the reason the rest of the band had appeared somewhat edgy that night. They hadn't been worried about breaking in a new band member, they just knew that our playing was intended to hide the noise of the work going on down below. I marvelled at how daring it was.

'Put these on,' said Dana, chucking me a set of blue overalls. 'We can't have you arriving home from band practice covered in dirt.'

Someone had slung a rope ladder over the side of the

hole, which made it possible to clamber down inside it relatively easily. I could see the separate layers as I made my way down. First the concrete floor, then beneath that a layer of looser stones, and finally the hard clay. There was something thrilling about standing there, looking up at Gerold and Dana peering over the edge above me. I couldn't believe that we were actually doing something. If we made it to the West, I might really get to see my mother and sister again.

A bucket and rope attached to a pulley hung next to the ladder and there was a pile of empty sandbags ready to remove the earth that was dug out. I wondered how much dirt they would be removing over the coming days and weeks – would there be enough space to hide it in this little warren of storerooms?

I crouched to look into the square opening of the tunnel, which came up to about my waist-height. A narrow passageway, just large enough to crawl through and for the workers to dig in, sloped downwards into the dark. I tried to imagine what it would be like to dig through the thick, heavy clay in such a confined area. I have never liked small spaces and the thought of having to spend hours in that cramped tunnel made me feel a little queasy. It must have been back-breaking work too.

The guys had been working around the clock since the night of that first gig and had made impressive progress. I wasn't sure how many people were involved in total, but Dana had explained that they were working in shifts to do the digging. Each shift was relatively short, only three or four hours. This meant the diggers were always fresh and that it wasn't noticeable that people were missing from their ordinary lives for too long. The café was the perfect cover for the groups of three men to come in and out. One person would be deep inside the tunnel digging and filling up sandbags with the dirt. The next followed behind, fitting the wooden struts to support the tunnel and dragging the heavy sandbags to the edge of the tunnel. Here, the final person shifted them up and out of the way. As the tunnel grew longer, there was a plan to add more men to each detail, so that the work wouldn't be held up by the slow speed at which the sandbags had to be manoeuvred in such tight confines.

Dana handed down a torch and I shone it into the darkness, but the tunnel was already too long for me to see the end. I turned back to Gerold and Dana, crouching at the edge of the hole.

'It's so impressive,' I said. 'I want to help.'

'We don't need you to do any of the digging,' said

Dana. I don't know if she could tell I was nervous about spending time in that confined space. 'You have plenty on your plate dealing with your Stasi dad.'

'No,' I said, suddenly determined. 'Put me on a shift. I can tell Hans I'm at rehearsal. I have to help.'

HARRY

There was only one place on Wilhelmstraße I could think of that would make a potential exit for a tunnel from the East. Beneath our own apartment building, just a stone's throw from the Wall, was a large basement. It was not accessible to the residents, but the *Hausmeister* – who was a mix of caretaker, security and front desk – definitely had a key. I just had to think of a way of getting him to let me take a look around.

When I knocked on his office, the *Hausmeister* seemed more taken with the soccer game he was listening to on his little radio than he was with helping me find my imaginary cat. I noted which key he took from its hook in the cabinet. The cabinet itself didn't look too secure. I was confident I could break into it if required. When the time came, I'd be able to sneak into the basement, then lock it from the inside and wait. I would listen for the sound of banging and scraping, and I would be there – the first face they would see welcoming them to the West. I would be the one to reach out a hand and help them through the hole.

The *Hausmeister* opened the basement door for me. There was a damp smell in there. I could hear the clack of pipes and boilers, the heartbeat of the building. I didn't need the torch I was clutching in my right hand. There was a bare bulb hanging from the ceiling, casting the corners in deep shadows. I stood in the doorway and the *Hausmeister* looked at me with irritation.

'*Mach schon*,' he said, nudging me in the back, almost shoving me into the basement. 'Hurry up.'

He stood in the doorway of the basement with his arms folded, tapping his foot in impatience while I called out 'Whiskers', because it was the first name I could think of. I was keen to look at the floor, to see visible signs of what could be broken. My steps were slow, deliberate. I needed time to take it all in so that I could describe it all to Jakob.

The space was dusty, with a damp smell that suggested the boilers were leaky. Along one wall were shelves of cleaning products, each gathering dust of their own. There was a spider or two. A mop leaning in the corner had dried out long ago.

'Whiskers, Whiskers, come here, *Kätzchen*.'

I was crouched low, almost on my hands and knees. The

basement was a concrete box. I couldn't see any way they could break through, not without specialist equipment. '*Raus mit dir, jetzt reicht's*,' barked the Hausmeister summoning me back. '*Hier ist keine Katze.*'

You've got that right, I thought. *There is no cat here.*

I walked over to him slowly, casting my eyes left and right.

'Just one more scout around,' I said. 'It won't take a second.'

I looked back into the room, desperate now. And that's when I spotted it. How could I have missed it before? The drain right in the middle of the floor.

I walked back over to it, and then to the wall, and back again slowly.

'Okay, done,' I said. 'You're right. *Hier ist kein Kätzchen.* '

The Hausmeister shrugged and acted like I had wasted his time. Locking the door, he muttered, '*Verrückte Amerikaner*,' under his breath. I thanked him and ran up to my bedroom again. Let him think I was a 'crazy American'. I'd be less suspicious that way.

It was ten steps from the drain to the wall.

That evening, I headed outside. It was warm and there was a buzz in the air. Laughter and voices came from the surrounding streets, the corner bars busy with people finished with work for the day. I was alone though, as I paced out the distance from my apartment to the Wall.

Fifty steps.

Safer to double-check.

Forty-nine steps. Plus the ten in the basement.

It was then I realised I was being watched by a man and a woman in tight, bright clothes on a nearby bench. He swigged a bottle of beer and she smoked a cigarette, blowing clouds from pursed lips. They looked so cool, like characters from a movie.

'What are you doing?' said the man in a German accent. People always seemed to guess I was a 'Yank' just by looking at me, although given that we were in the heart of the American Sector, maybe that was to be expected. 'Don't tell me you're measuring out an escape into the East? That would be suicide, no?'

And he laughed and looked at his girlfriend for a response, but all she did was look at me and look away, detached, before she carried on smoking her cigarette.

I stood rooted to the spot.

'No,' I mumbled to him. 'Science project.'

Thankfully, the night was too dark for them to see me blush.

'A science project,' he laughed and took another swig. 'Hey, Einstein, what's it like being a genius?'

The woman stubbed out her cigarette on the ground and turned to him. She kissed him on the mouth and said something in German which I took to mean 'let's go'. They quickly got up and left, leaving me alone on that Berlin street.

Back in my room I scribbled my reply to Jakob.

Dear Jakob,
Thank you for your letter. I was delighted to hear your news.
It's unbelievable, like something from the movies! Of course, I will help in any way I can.
My parents are settling in fine.
It's been fascinating to discover a new city.
There is a safe place for you to surface in the basement of my apartment building.
I'm so jealous that you get to play with a real band.
I have paced it out and it is forty-nine paces from the Wall, which works out at about a hundred and ten feet.
I'd love to hear more about The Stamp Collectors.
If you break into the sewer at that point, you'll be able to come in through the grate.
I'd love to hear you play live one day.
I'm sure we can find you a gig once you all arrive!
Nobody goes in there so there will be no one to get suspicious about any noise.
Do write soon and let me know how you're all getting along.

Your friend,

Harry

I thought about mentioning Marie, how she'd agreed to help with the search for his mother, but I decided against it. I didn't know how to explain how I'd met her because I didn't want to tell him what had happened to Dieter. How I had been responsible.

The difficult part was coming up with a believable message to write in ink. The truth was, I was kind of jealous of his life, especially getting to play with a band. He had been wrenched from his family, but how I would have loved to have friends like he did. Back in D.C., we'd sometimes played at being superheroes, Mike, Robbie and I. It seemed childish to me now, but I had to admit, I missed those times.

I sealed the envelope and imagined coming face to face with Jakob.

I hoped he would make it.

As I lay in bed that night thinking it all over, I wondered whether, if worst came to worst, I could call on Dad for help. He worked for the West, after all. Despite what had happened to Dieter and his store, what my dad had done to him, I wanted to believe Dad still had a good heart. He was just trying in his own way to protect me.

The truth was, I barely saw my dad any more. Spending most of my afternoons at Dieter's store meant that I wasn't at home all that much. My dad was spending less time at home too. He'd started coming back later and later, and often locked himself up in his office when he was around. Dinners were made by my mom and left to stand on the counter for him to reheat later.

I spent most evenings shut up in my bedroom listening to rock and roll, tuning the dial through the fuzz and interference in search of the familiar sound of a guitar, a drumbeat, a voice. One night, the batteries died in my radio. I could have kicked myself for not picking up some spares. I lay awake for a while, staring at the ceiling and trying to stop my mind from thinking about Jakob and his mother, about Dieter, about the boy on the Wall. It was gone midnight when I heard music coming from inside our apartment. It was the piano in the study; my dad playing a strange sequence of notes. A hesitant, repeated pattern that didn't seem to fit any key that I knew.

I had never known him to touch the piano before, and I assumed he'd drunk too much Bourbon. He certainly didn't seem very good at it.

Two nights later, as I was lying in bed trying to sleep, I heard what sounded like the same music being played again. The night after that, the same – a seemingly random sequence of notes. When curiosity finally got the better of me the following morning, I asked him about it, but he was dismissive.

'So I play the damn piano while I'm trying to think about work. So what?'

It just seemed so strange, my dad playing the piano. Sure, he liked music. He loved the ballrooms of the 40s and 50s, but he had never seemed interested in playing an instrument like I did. And it sounded too weird, more than just messing around. It was the fact that it seemed to be the same sequence of notes played at the same speed over and over. At first, I figured he was trying to teach himself and he was too embarrassed to tell me, or even ask for my help.

At least, that's what I thought. But then, a couple of nights later, something even more bizarre happened. I was listening to my radio when the song just stopped and there was nothing for a moment, just the fuzz of white noise. Then, slowly coming through – faint at first and then audible – the same notes that Dad had played on the piano. I was almost certain it was the exact same sequence.

I woke up the next morning still wondering, the notes going around in my head. Dad had already left for the day and the apartment was silent. Mom was lying in longer and longer in the mornings.

I had a mission to complete. I felt like The Fly as I took a paper clip from my desk and straightened it out to make one long strand. I wasn't an expert lock-picker, but my cousin Ben had shown me a technique once, which he used to break into his sister's room. The lock on the study door wasn't a good one and I managed to work the paperclip into the keyhole, tripping the mechanism. The door swung open.

I hadn't been in here since Dad had cancelled my piano lessons following his blow-up over that phone call he'd taken when I'd been playing. I think it was supposed to be a punishment, which showed just how little he knew me – it was actually a relief not to have to spend any more time with the tedious Herr Müller. I hadn't really felt the urge to play piano at all recently.

Dad hadn't been keeping the office tidy since then. There was paperwork strewn all over his desk. I didn't know what I was looking for, just any clue that might explain what he'd been doing. I ran my hands along the closed lid of the piano first, checked all around for signs of anything strange, but there was nothing. Then I turned my attention to the desk. My German wasn't good enough to read the documents that were left out and I was scared to take anything away with me to try and translate later in case my dad noticed.

I was feeling disheartened at the failure of my mission, when I noticed a photograph pinned to the board of memos above the desk. It was half-obscured by a newspaper cutting of some dinner Dad had attended when he arrived in Berlin, but there was no mistaking what it was. It was a picture of the Wall that seemed to have been taken from a window in our apartment. But what was surprising was the moment that it captured. The photo had been snapped at the moment the dead boy had been caught in the barbed wire. I could see the American guards gathered around and could even make out myself, stood slightly back and staring. It all rushed back to me. The shouting. The gunshots. The look on the boy's face. I felt dizzy.

I took a deep breath and glanced out of the study window towards the Wall. I tried to work out what angle the picture had been taken from. And how and why had it worked its way into my father's hands?

I leant over the desk to look for anything else in the photograph. As I shuffled forwards, trying to get a better look, I felt my foot nudge something beneath the desk. I found a small briefcase in the shadows. I knelt down to open it, but it was locked. I knocked the back of my head hard on the bottom of the desk as I tried to stand up and fell forwards on the floor again, feeling embarrassed even though I was on my own.

It was from that position, sprawled on the floor, that I noticed the small key taped to the back leg of the desk. It was almost too easy, but then, my father probably hadn't really expected anyone to break into his office. I gently unpeeled the Scotch tape, took out the briefcase and put the key in the lock. I don't know what I felt when I saw that it matched, when I heard the click as it turned. I wavered, wondering if I should open it. If I saw something I didn't want to, there would be no going back.

And then I reminded myself I had come this far for a reason. I couldn't let my memories of happier times stop me from getting to the bottom of what was going on now. I wouldn't be able to fix anything with my dad if I didn't even know what it was that needed fixing. I thought about what The Fly would do.

Inside the briefcase I found a radio transmitter with numerous dials and tubes, along with some kind of microphone and a small beige book. I picked up the latter and leafed through the pages. They each contained music staves with a strange notation. It looked like it might be in a code of some sort, perhaps each note relating to a letter in the alphabet? I was about to look up the notes my dad had been playing when I heard a movement from my parents' room.

As I closed the notebook, I noticed the emblem on the front for the first time. The hammer and compass of the GDR. I was rushing, but even so, that caused me to pause. Why did my father, my senior American diplomat father, have a notebook of East German codes? Was he just trying to decipher them? Surely they had other people to do that kind of work? I could think of only one kind of person that used codes like this. It was how spies passed messages back and forth in comic books.

I felt lightheaded as I locked the book back in the case. My hands were trembling as I stuck the key back to the leg of the table using the small piece of tape. I slipped out of the study and headed to my room to try and work things out. It was only when I heard the shower running that I remembered to go back to lock the door again with my trusty paperclip. I knew I would be needing it again soon.

JAKOB

My first and only shift of digging came four days after Dana and Gerold had shown me the tunnel. Viktor had hurt his wrist the day before, so the digging team for that afternoon was a man down. The idea of crawling through the tight confines of the tunnel sent a shiver down my spine, but I couldn't bear the idea of not helping when I was needed. So, under cover of a 'rehearsal', I made my way down to the basement in the company of Ralf and Cristopher.

I tried not to show my nerves in front of the others as we headed down the basement stairs. We all got changed out of our clothes and into the overalls that were hanging on hooks on the wall. We would be able to clean ourselves up using the sink in the kitchen upstairs, but our clothes would need to look clean when we left. I folded mine carefully, remembering it was Margot who would be washing them that evening.

Clambering down into the hole, the tunnel seemed even smaller than before. My heart was racing and my hands felt clammy as Cristopher led the way on all fours. I noticed a damp odour in the air as I took a deep breath and followed him in. There was hardly enough room for me to crawl, and I was quite a bit smaller than the others. It felt like the walls were closing in as I inched deeper and deeper, clutching my torch. I kept knocking my elbows on the wooden struts and the wall scraped along my back.

'Everything OK?' called Ralf. He was waiting back in the room, ready to lift the sandbags I was supposed to be dragging out.

'All good,' Cristopher called back.

I could feel the panic rise inside me as we made our way deeper into the dark. It took all my determination to keep following Cristopher down that tunnel, but finally we came to the end. I breathed in and out slowly to try and settle my nerves, as Cristopher somehow manoeuvred himself to lie on his back with his feet towards the end wall. Then he took hold of a spade that had been left there by the last crew and dug in that position, using his feet to push the spade into the dirt. He tipped each spadeful into a bag at his side.

It was hard work and Cristopher was soon sweating, despite the cool of the earth around us. As he filled each bag, I would lean over him to drag it back, feeling his hot breath on my face. I then had to drag the heavy sandbag full of earth backwards out of the tunnel to give to Ralf, before returning to Cristopher for the next load. It was back-breaking work and I wasn't even doing any of the heavy digging.

Halfway through our three-hour shift Cristopher and I crawled out of the tunnel and stretched ourselves out. For the second half, Ralf headed into the tunnel to take up the digging, while Cristopher stayed outside to lift the sandbags. Nobody suggested I should do any work with the pickaxe or spade and I knew enough not to volunteer. It was all I could do to keep up the pace dragging the sandbags out. It seemed such an unimportant job, but as my arms were aching dragging bag after bag to the tunnel entrance, I realised that without me clearing away the dirt, the whole process would have been much slower. It was only with everyone doing their small part that we might all be able to escape.

I was exhausted by the time Gerold came down to tell us our shift was over. As he led the way back up to the café for us to wash up, Ralf showed me his hands. They were patterned with black and blue bruises and little cuts from the digging.

'And Dana still expects me to be the best drummer in East Berlin,' he said, laughing.

'It's all right for you drummers,' said Cristopher from a little further ahead. 'Try getting your fingering right on an accordion with blisters all over your hands.'

HARRY

At first, I refused to believe that my dad could be a spy for the Communists. I was reading too much into that symbol. His job was to defend the West against the East Germans, that's why he had one of their codebooks. But why would he have been given that kind of task? What business did an American diplomat have with GDR codes?

It would explain a lot. How distant he had become and how angry he would get over small things like a comic book. It would also explain why he punished Dieter by having him sent away. If my dad was working for the East, then he would think of Dieter as the traitor.

I wondered what could have driven him to it. Dad had never seemed motivated by money, so I didn't think they could have offered him that. I thought back on his little speeches about 'the West'. My dad had always seemed like a patriotic man. That's why he had gone into politics.

Then again, his speeches had only begun about two years before, back in Washington. At the time, I hadn't thought all that much about them; everyone seemed to make speeches in Washington. But looking back, there was something odd about the way he spoke sometimes. As if he was reciting lines. Had they already gotten to him back then? Did they know something about his past that Mom and I didn't know? Or had they brainwashed him? There were plenty of movies about very clever men turning against their country.

At least he didn't seem to know about my own contact with the East. If he ever discovered that, it wouldn't just mean trouble for me – Jakob could be in real danger.

Jakob's latest letter had arrived within a week of my last one to him.

Dear Harry,

It was so great to hear from you as always.

Great work finding a safe exit point for us. It was very clever of you to pace out the distances and Gerold has been able to plot everything on our map.

I'm so glad your parents are well.

Please don't give up looking for my mother and sister, but be careful — don't do or say anything that could give us away.

The band is doing great, we're starting to sound really good in rehearsals and I hope we may even be able to record one or two of our songs for broadcast soon.

You should see the tunnel! It's really a remarkable thing. It must already stretch most of the way to the Wall and we're working in shifts to get it finished.

I would love for you to see us play live one day.

It may be a few weeks yet, but I will let you know when to expect us.

Stay in touch.

Yours,

Jakob

I stood at my bedroom window after reading it, watching night fall over the East. I imagined Jakob and his friends tunnelling under that street as the border guards walked around above without a clue. It didn't seem real, somehow. I lost myself in thought standing there and suddenly realised that my dad had started playing that strange music in his study again. I felt sick in the pit of my stomach.

I watched my dad more closely over the next week. I was looking for a change, for a crack in his armour.

At breakfast, I watched him chewing his cooked breakfast. I wondered if he had always pushed the bacon to one side of the plate and left it until last to eat.

'What are you staring at?'

'Nothing.' I shrugged, shifting my gaze to my Cheerios,

a taste from back home that had appeared in the kitchen cupboard that week.

After he had left for work, in the time before I headed out to school, I pulled out the paperclip and broke into the study again. I had a quick look around, checking if anything had changed since I was last there. Then I opened the briefcase and settled down to my task, carefully copying out the first third or so of the codebook. I thought about sneaking it out of his office so I could continue my work at school, but decided it wasn't worth the risk. In truth, I didn't really understand what it was I was copying out and of course the codes were meaningless unless I could find the messages they related to. But I was sure the piano playing had something to do with it.

And then, it just stopped. I hadn't heard it for a week or so and I was getting nowhere poring over my notes about the code. I began to feel like I was wasting my time. If anything, my dad was back to his old self. He was still distant, but there were no further outbursts. I felt bad for my suspicions, for questioning what he was doing.

The worst thing was that I hadn't heard from Jakob either. What if he was in trouble? What if he had been discovered? I knew that there were often delays with the mail, especially crossing the border, but I couldn't bear the tension.

I just wanted something to happen. I should have been careful what I wished for.

JAKOB

The Stamp Collectors were sitting around a table in the back room of Café Bruno, their faces long and drawn and serious. My first thought, inexplicably, was that this was some kind of practical joke, but then I saw Gerold, his elbows on the counter and fresh tears on his cheeks.

'What's happened?'

No one seemed able to speak. Ralf wouldn't meet my gaze; he fiddled with his moustache. Cristopher stared into the distance. Nadine looked terrified.

I managed to catch her eye, pointed downwards and mouthed, 'The tunnel?' She shook her head and gave a nervous laugh. She turned to Viktor and indicated with her hand that he should tell me. But even Viktor – steady Viktor, whose trombone never hit a duff note – was dumbstruck. His mouth hung open.

And then I didn't need anyone to explain.

'Where is she?'

The floodgates opened. Everyone spoke at once.

'We don't know ...'

'They took her ...'

'Last night ...'

I couldn't hear, couldn't understand. I shushed them with a wave of my hand.

'Who took her?'

Gerold took the lead. He came out from behind the counter, took my hand in his and said the very words I did not want to hear.

'The Stasi.'

With that, my stomach sank. Gerold continued. 'They visited her this morning. They went to Dana's apartment and they took her. One of her neighbours heard. They told her they wanted to take her in for routine questioning on matters of vital state security. The usual excuses.' He shook his head sadly.

'I should have been there,' said Cristopher.

'And if you'd been there, what would you have done?' asked Ralf.

'Do they know about the tunnel?' I asked.

'If they knew about the tunnel, none of us would be here,' responded Ralf. His face was white, and I began to understand – they were scared, not just for Dana, but for themselves. All of them – except perhaps Gerold, who seemed to be more sad than afraid.

Viktor gave Ralf a disappointed look. Then he turned back to me. 'Our first thoughts were the same as yours,' he said. 'We came straight here. Thought we'd try to remove any evidence, protect Gerold. But no. The Stasi seemed to have other interests in her. She has other friends, family. Perhaps some suspicion has fallen on them.'

'But she does know about the tunnel,' Ralf said. 'And the Stasi have her.'

'Dana would never betray us,' I said. I was certain that was true. 'She's worked so hard for it. Never.'

After a moment, Gerold spoke, softly. 'You know, Jakob, there are things the Stasi can do – terrible, inhuman things. Even Dana might not be able to hold out.'

I knew more than I wanted to about the Stasi's methods. There were always rumours swirling around at school about what happened to the people who were picked up for questioning. Whilst Jürgen was a good friend, I found his interest in these interrogation techniques weird. Usually so dismissive of our fathers' work, he became almost gleeful when discussing the Stasi's use of solitary confinement, starvation or violence. It was Jürgen who had told me about Hans' reputation too. His father reported that, even amongst the Stasi, my adopted father was well known for his ability to interrogate. I didn't like to think about it, but I could well believe it.

I had a sudden, awful vision of Dana alone in a cell in the *Hohenschönhausen* – the Stasi prison in the Lichtenberg district of Berlin. She would have been blindfolded on the way in so that she wouldn't be able to give away the location if they ever let her out. In my vision, they had taken away Dana's glasses, and her uncovered eyes stared out into the blackness. There was no one there to comfort her, not even other prisoners to talk to. Fear wrapped itself around my stomach.

'We have to get her out,' I said. 'We have to do something.'

'Do something?' said Ralf. 'Do what? Are you not listening, Jakob? Are you that naïve? The Stasi have arrested her. There's nothing we can do.' His voice strained higher and higher. Nadine placed a finger on the back of his hand to silence him, but the fear was all over her face too.

'Why did they pick her up – that's what I want to know,' said Cristopher. He obviously thought someone from the group must have said something.

'Don't,' said Gerold, casting him a warning look.

'I mean, it's not as if any of us have a close connection

with the Stasi, is it,' he said, looking at me. I could feel the heat rising in my face. I wanted to defend myself, but he was right. However much I hated it, Hans was my adopted father.

'There is something I can do,' I said.

I needed to prove that I was with them. And I needed to do something to help Dana.

The walk from Café Bruno to Ruschestraße was over an hour, but I have no recollection of that journey at all. Which route did I take? Did I look as I crossed the road? I cannot say. I remember that final look of fear and trepidation on the faces of The Stamp Collectors. I had seen it before, though not for many years. The look my parents had, the day we tried to flee.

I remember the faces of the band, and then I remember being in front of Stasi HQ.

Above me were eight rows of white windows embedded in grey concrete. A slow trickle of suited people scurried in and out of the building, nodding occasional polite greetings to one another. Cars – nondescript, normal cars – filed down into an underground car park. There was a guard post, but nothing else to indicate that this innocuous office building was the source of so much fear.

As I watched, the guard shifted his rifle from one shoulder to the other.

'Hey, kid!' The guard shouted from his post. 'What are you staring at?' I became aware that I had been stood there a while, trying to gain enough courage to approach. I walked towards him.

'I'm here to see my father,' I said. 'He works here.'

'That so? Well, maybe best you see him at home. He's probably busy at work, hmm?' The guard had bags under his eyes and his tone was weary and cynical.

'My father,' I repeated. 'Hans Eberhardt.'

The guard gulped. With grim satisfaction, I entered the building.

Hans' office was on the fifth floor. A secretary, a skeletal man in his sixties, led me up in the lift. Where the outside and the reception area had been busy, the corridors up here were quiet, and lined with worn beige carpet. We had to wait outside the office for ten minutes. I told the secretary he could leave me there, but he shook his head. He didn't say a word the whole time.

Eventually, the door cracked open. A bald man in a shirt and loose necktie stumbled out, gave me the once-over, then headed off.

'Jakob!' said Hans. He smiled a fake smile and shook

my hand. As always, his grip was fiercely tight. 'What on earth are you doing here? Is everything well at school?'

'It's not about school, it's about—'

But before I could finish, he ushered me in with a quick look down the corridor and a dismissive flick of his hand to the secretary.

His office was not large: a desk, a metal filing cabinet, a coat-stand with his long mac hanging from it. He sat behind the desk and sat me in the single chair in front of it, which was small and wooden and not especially comfortable. On his desk was a telephone and a pair of manila folders, set to one side. Both folders had some kind of code written on them – a six-digit number in black marker, and a purple stamp:

CONFIDENTIALITY LEVEL 2
AUTHORISED PERSONNEL ONLY

'What are you doing here?' Hans repeated. 'It's pleasant to see you, of course. I've a busy day, though, many things to which I must attend.'

'It's Dana.'

'Your friend from orchestra? What about her?' His expression was puzzled. If he knew something about Dana, he was good at hiding it.

'She was arrested. This morning.'

'Arrested.' He said it with no inflection, like he was saying 'bread' or 'road'. 'Hold on.' He picked up the telephone and turned the dial once, letting it ratchet back. 'I need the files on Dana Decker ... D – E – C – K – E – R ... Yes ... Yes, all of them.'

It struck me as odd that he knew Dana's full name. Had he done background checks on her? I'd never considered that before. I felt a chill go down my neck at the idea that he might do research on everyone I met.

Within a few minutes, another folder was in his hands. He leaned back in his chair and opened it. I couldn't see the contents. The folder was only marked as confidentiality level 3, and I took some comfort from the fact that there were apparently more serious cases.

He shut the file and looked across at me.

'What is it you want to know?'

'Why has she been arrested? On what grounds are you holding her?'

'You know I can't divulge information like that.'

'But she hasn't done anything wrong. She's innocent.'

'And how would you know that? Has she told you something?'

'No!' I said quickly. 'No, but I know she wouldn't do anything wrong.'

Hans sucked his lips in. 'And how do you know that, Jakob? How long have you known her, after all? People can be very convincing when they want to be. Believe me. It's my job to find out when people are lying.'

'But Dana's not lying.'

He gave his joyless shark's smile. 'Yet you are.'

'Wh – what do you mean?'

'I'm impressed with your loyalty to your friends, Jakob. It is a good trait. A sign that you will go far one day. But I know, and I think you know, that Dana is not entirely innocent. I don't think she's anyone important. I don't think she has done anything terribly wrong. But I think she might know someone who *has* done something wrong, or someone who will. Tell me what you know about Café Bruno.'

The air thickened about us. The muffled quiet of the office deepened. A flicker of sunshine through the window blurred my vision. I knew I had to think quickly, but my thoughts were like tar.

'I – I have heard some talk there, yes. Dangerous talk, maybe. But nothing that unusual. Nothing I haven't heard before in the playground.' I felt as if I was on a tightrope across a canyon, trying to not look down or show any sign of weakness.

'The playground?' Hans made a note on his pad, gave a tuneless whistle. 'It's not talk I am interested in, Jakob. I am not as out of touch as you might think. I know the kind of things people say. It is useful for you to hear these things. To understand what we are up against. But Jakob, I trust you to avoid saying these things yourself. For talk leads to actions – and it is actions that I want to know about. Have you seen anything, noticed anything out of the ordinary at Café Bruno? This man, this' – he consulted the file – 'this Gerold Klug, for instance. What about him?'

Gerold? Gerold was in their files? Kind, generous Gerold? The confusion must have played across my face, but Hans betrayed nothing. He just looked at me steadily. Waited until I found myself speaking.

'I don't know much about him. We've only spoken once or twice. But I could find out more.' I felt like I was betraying Gerold just by saying it, but I had to buy more time. Hans' eyes closed and when they opened again, he nodded.

'Could you, Jakob? Find out more, and tell me more?'

'Yes,' I said. 'I have heard talk there. From some of the regulars. Perhaps there is more.'

Hans leaned back and folded his hands. 'Good, Jakob.'

'But I want Dana released.' At the mention of the 'want'

Hans' eyes tightened. I hurried on. 'Otherwise, I fear, everyone at the café will be too suspicious to talk to me. They are already very suspicious of me. They know who my adop— who my father is. I'm very new there, as you said. If we want them to tell me more, if there is something more to find out, Dana will need to be released.'

Hans drummed his fingers on the desk once, then pointed at me. 'You're right, Jakob. You're exactly right.' His grey eyes seemed to drill into me. 'You have so much promise, Jakob. So much talent. Yes, we'll release Dana, and then I'll rely on you to bring me more information.' He shook his head. 'So much promise. We don't talk of it often in our house, for it makes your mother uncomfortable, but we know we are not your biological parents. And yet – you remind me of myself when I was younger. One day, Jakob, I think you will surpass me.'

I turned away so he wouldn't see the anger on my face. *I'm nothing like you!* I wanted to scream. But I swallowed the words.

I noticed someone out of the corner of my eye as I left the building. It looked like Cristopher. I thought perhaps he had come to find out how I got on talking to Hans, but as I turned towards him he disappeared around the corner. I wasn't even sure that it was him, but something about the incident made me feel uneasy.

I told myself many things in the hours and days that followed. I told myself that I was doing it for the greater good. That I was only pretending to inform on my friends. I told myself that I would use my position to buy time for The Stamp Collectors.

But I knew what I was doing was dangerous. Not just for me, but for everyone involved.

That night Hans and Margot kept sharing beaming looks over the dinner table. I half-expected them to whip out my 'Informal Collaborator' file, detailing all the people I was willing to give evidence against, and start cooing over it as if it was a photo of me as a baby. Margot made what she thought was my favourite food – *Apfelstrudel*. In the first few days following my father's arrest and my mother's defection, I had made the mistake of telling a friendly female government official that I loved *Apfelstrudel*. Now it was Margot's sure-fire way to reward me if I did something she approved of. Every bite tasted like mud to me.

Dana was released from her cell that very evening, Hans clearly had a great deal of power in such matters. I went to see her first thing the next morning. She wore black that day, and her face was wan and puffy. We hugged, then she led me to the kitchen, where she had a plate of untouched scrambled eggs on the table.

Gerold had given me the address to Dana's apartment. I knew she lived here with her mother, who was often out at work. The kitchen was joined to a living area with a couple of beaten-up leather sofas. A door led to her bedroom. A poster on the wall for *Der Hund von Baskerville*. It was tidy but not spotless – I noticed the washing-up was piled in the sink.

'Did they hurt you?' I asked, but she put a warning finger up to her lips, then went over to the record player. She put on a recording of a classical concerto and turned the volume up loud enough to mask our conversation.

'They have been in here.' She looked warily around the room. 'They will have bugs somewhere.'

'What happened?' I whispered, matching her hushed tone.

'Frau Albert. Next door. I think she told them.'

'About Café Bruno? How does she know?'

'No. They don't know about any of that. They didn't ask me about it.'

'Then ... why?'

'I – I still don't know, not really.'

She suspected someone must have spoken to the Stasi, suggested that she was not as loyal as she seemed. She had heard a knock on the door early in the morning, just before seven, while it was still dark. There were two of them – a man and a woman. They were dressed in plain clothes, but she knew they were Stasi right away. 'They just had that look,' she said. 'Dead eyes.' They asked if she wouldn't mind coming along with them to their offices to answer a few questions. They were friendly to start with, almost exaggeratedly polite. They asked her questions about her work, her studies. They knew things about her – what grades she had got, where she had applied to teacher training, her sister's address. And then they started asking more general questions – did she ever hear anyone criticise the GDR? Or the leadership of the GDR? She said nothing, just spoke vaguely about loyalty to the state.

'No. I haven't heard anything.'

'No. Nobody I know talks like that.'

Then the questions got more personal. They asked about her friends and about Café Bruno.

She tried to explain that they were all in a band. That there was nothing improper going on. A look had passed between her interrogators. Then they had said that they wanted to ask her some more questions. But later. She was taken to a room to stew.

'They led me down this long corridor with cells either side, maybe thirty in total. The doors were all metal, so I couldn't see whether there was anybody in the other ones. My cell was tiny – just a cot and a toilet. The light switch and the toilet flush were both on the outside. They just left me there. There was nothing to do. Nothing to read. When they turned the light off, the only light left was from a small window made of glass bricks. I just lay on the bed and thought about things. The tunnel. The band, the orchestra. Other things. I started thinking about those princesses from history that were locked away in towers, all on their own, for years and years and years.' Her eyes were far away. Then she gave a snort. 'How weak. They just put me in a room for a few hours, on my own and it broke me.'

'It didn't break you,' I said. But she didn't acknowledge me, she just carried on with her story.

'Then they released me. Just like that. No explanation. No apology. "Here's your bag, here's your clothes." They drove me back to the apartment in a windowless van. The way they looked at me ... it was like I was an object, like I wasn't even there.' She lifted a piece of toast up to her mouth, then put it back on the plate, untouched. 'The funny thing is, I don't even blame them. The people who work there. They're just doing a job. It's the system that's the problem. I see it now, more clearly than before.' She sighed and asked me, 'Jakob, are you all right? You look worried. Not about me, I hope? I'm fine, really.'

I had not meant to look worried, and I kicked myself mentally. I was playing a dangerous game now, a game of deception that people's lives depended upon, and I needed to get better at hiding my emotions. But I also needed to tell Dana. After what she'd been through, I felt I owed it to her.

'It was me. I got you released. I spoke to Hans.'

'You? Oh, Jakob. Thank you.' She leaned over to kiss my cheek. I backed out of reach. 'You don't understand, Dana. You don't know what Hans is like. I had to give him something in return.'

A crease furrowed Dana's brow.

'I had to agree to become an informant for the Stasi. I said I would inform on any suspicious activities at the Café.' The danger of what I was doing, the peril I had put myself and my new friends in suddenly caught up with me. My voice cracked. 'They are not far behind us.'

I expected her to be angry. A part of me wanted some sort of outlet for the guilt I felt at what I had promised to do, at how I had compromised myself. But if she was angry, she didn't express it. She said, 'You did what you had to do, Jakob. Even you, even me – we are part of the system. It's what it does to people.'

For a moment, she just looked sad, as if the weight of all the GDR was on her, all its crimes, all its million lies placed upon her shoulders. But then she brightened.

'One thing's for sure – we're going to have to dig quicker.'

HARRY

Usually, at night, I heard the sound of doors opening and closing twice. The first time, when my dad went into the study after his dinner. Then again, gone midnight, when he went to the bedroom, where my mother was already asleep. But, just as life seemed to be settling into a routine again, there was one night when I didn't hear the usual sounds.

I was eating my breakfast the next morning when I saw Dad leave the study looking dishevelled. He glanced down the corridor and noticed me staring, then locked the door, taking his time, being deliberate with the key.

He had a glass of water at the kitchen sink and left for work without saying a word or changing his clothes. I had never seen him leave without taking a shower before.

I waited ten minutes before steeling myself to go to the study. I fumbled with the paperclip, trying to get it to trip the lock, but something was wrong. The paperclip was bending too much as I twisted it. The scratching noise seemed to echo in the empty hall and I began to worry that it would wake my mother. Finally, just as I was about to give up, I felt it give and the door swung open.

The room was even more messy than usual. As I approached the desk, I noticed some new additions on top of it – a detailed street map of Berlin, including both sides of the Wall, and a tape recorder. Picking up the recorder, I turned the volume down so that my mom wouldn't hear from her room. The tape was of some classical music that my dad must have recorded from the radio. I knew it was the radio because of the programmer's voice between the tracks. A slightly gruff German voice that mentioned the name of the orchestra and the piece being played; it wasn't anything I had heard of. He also said something about the recording coming from the Funkhaus Nalepastraße. I knew that place. Jakob had mentioned it. It was a big concert venue or something over in the East.

I listened for a while. It was suspicious that my dad would have recorded this from the radio. It wasn't the kind of thing he liked to listen to. This was a full orchestra, playing some old classical piece. I was about to press the stop button when the music finished abruptly. It seemed to have been cut off before its natural end, and then a piece of piano music began to play. A strange and familiar sound.

The piano notes were so like the ones Dad had played in the study. They had to be related in some way. Another message sent in the same code.

I went under the desk and retrieved the key. I dragged the briefcase out and opened it. Nestled inside was the code book I was looking for, but beneath it was a dark green notebook. When I opened it, I saw that the entries were in my dad's handwriting. I couldn't believe it – he had written out the messages! Part of me was annoyed to have wasted so many hours trying to work out this code if my dad was stupid enough to leave the transcribed messages lying around. Mostly, though, I was sickened by the lists of names and addresses, presumably belonging to people the East wanted watched. There were so many, I didn't know where to start. This was what he had been doing in here on so many late nights. I felt sick with disappointment, but at least now I knew I had been right to doubt him. He was a Stasi spy!

I was so absorbed in my discovery that I didn't notice my mom get up and start moving around. I held my breath as she walked right past the study door on her way to the bathroom. I wondered if she already knew, if she had been in on whatever Dad was up to from the start. I thought about asking her, but I couldn't risk my dad finding out.

Instead, when we met in the kitchen later that morning, I asked her if she could bake an apple pie so we could all sit and eat dinner together when Dad got home. I wanted to see how they behaved in each other's company. She agreed and even managed a small smile.

That afternoon was the first time I had spent more than a few minutes alone with my mom in a long time. We had often baked together back in Washington, but it wasn't something I'd thought about since arriving in Berlin. I almost managed to forget about everything else as we prepared the apples and rolled out the pastry. That familiar smell of baking soon filled the apartment.

My dad arrived at seven and saw us sitting at the kitchen table. The food was growing cold, but still edible.

'Well, isn't this a pleasant surprise,' he said, but he didn't smile. The sharp sound of his chair being dragged under the table went right through me. We ate in silence. Both of my parents seemed to be concentrating on their food, although in my mom's case, this mostly involved pushing it around her plate. I wanted to say something, to let my dad know how betrayed I felt, but I couldn't give myself away. Not yet. It seemed as if we'd go a whole meal without a word being said, but as my mom served the pie, my dad finally spoke up.

'I won't be home on Friday night,' he said. 'I have some work to do with colleagues in the British Sector. We have a hotel. We're going to work through the night.'

Mom forced a smile. She did not serve a slice of pie for herself.

'The British Sector,' I said. 'Pretty cool. What will you be doing?'

'Just work stuff, Harry. Just work. Confidential, most of it ... it's to do with a speech the President needs to make.'

It felt like a lie. But what if I was wrong? Despite everything I'd seen, I still wanted to believe there could be an innocent explanation for things.

'Is there anything you want to talk about, Dad?'

'Nothing, why?' he said, forking his food like he had a vendetta against it.

'Are you sure there's nothing troubling you? Nothing you want to get off your chest?'

'What are you talking about, Harry? You sound like the Stasi or something, with all these questions.' With that, he pushed his chair back, got up and left the room. I heard his study door slam. He'd hardly touched his pie.

The next morning, I waited for him to leave for work and stole back into his study. I located the same notebook I'd seen the day before and started looking through it again. This time, I had a better idea what to look for. It didn't take much searching – the final page of notes had Friday's date and an address scribbled in my dad's handwriting.

Eberhardt meet confirmed, Ruschestraße 103.

It took me a moment to register the name. Eberhardt. Why did I know it? And then a feeling of dread settled upon me. Eberhardt, Hans Eberhardt. Jakob's adopted father.

I flattened out the map of Berlin he had on his desk. As I suspected, I couldn't find a *Ruschestraße* in the British Sector, so I studied the street names around the Wall. Sure enough, there it was, right in the heart of East Berlin.

Things happened fast after that. I was pretty sure my dad's meeting was with Jakob's father. If that was the case, perhaps he had information that he wanted to pass on in person. The Stasi had spies everywhere. They could monitor phone calls and use tiny recording devices called 'bugs' to record conversations. What if Café Bruno, or one of The Stamp Collectors had turned up in their files, in that tangled string of messages and codes?

I had four days to get myself together before my dad's meeting in the East. If, as I suspected, the Stasi had already got wind of the tunnel they were digging, it was up to me to try and get Jakob out.

I remembered a story Dieter had told me about a group who managed to evade detection inside a refrigerated van. They had hidden beneath a load of pork being transported to the West. As my dad already had permission to enter the East, I would hide myself in the trunk of his car, where I hoped nobody would bother looking. If I made it, I would try and bring Jakob back with me by the same route. The risks were huge, but I had to try.

I sent my final letter to Jakob.

Dear Jakob,

I just wanted to reach out as I haven't heard from you this week.

You were right to tell me to be cautious. I have discovered something important, which I must discuss with you in person.

I hope all is well with you and The Stamp Collectors. Do write and let me know how you're all getting along.

I have found a way into the East. Please meet me at your favourite cafe at 11 a.m. on Friday.

All the best,

Harry

JAKOB

My first reaction on reading Harry's latest letter? 'Idiot.'

I muttered the word under my breath in the toilet cubicle at the Funkhaus, hoping no one would smell the burning of the matches I had used to reveal the text. With everything that had been going on, I had only managed to reply to Harry a couple of days before, so I had been surprised to find another letter in Hans and Margot's postbox that morning. I'd been running late, so I shoved it in my backpack and headed off. When I arrived at the Funkhaus, Andi, the recording engineer, had been half-asleep in the booth.

'Oh, man, what time is it?'

'Late night?' I asked.

'Very.' He gave a close-lipped, tired smile. 'Just go and set up the mics in there, would you?' He rested his head in his hand for a second and then looked up again.

'Actually, Jakob, how would you feel about taking charge of the recording this morning? I'm not so feeling so well. Herr Christian's been saying I should give you more responsibility, anyway. I'll just sit here and watch.'

It was the first time I'd been allowed to be in charge of a recording session and in my excitement, I forgot all about Harry's letter. We had a string quartet in who were cutting a recording of Schubert's No. 14 for radio broadcast. I thought they'd see straightaway that I didn't really know what I was doing, but perhaps I'd picked up more than I realised after all the time I'd spent in the studios. They didn't even comment on my age or lack of experience. It was only when we took a break after an hour or so that I remembered the letter. I went to read in the toilet, swiping a pack of Andi's matches from the side.

I couldn't believe what I was reading. Harry was planning on trying to get to the East. It was madness. Did he know what he was risking? If the authorities found him, they would force him to tell them everything. He would be deported and get the rest of us sent to a Stasi prison – and that was a best-case scenario, for him and us.

I looked at my watch. His letter said he would be at Café Bruno at 11 a.m. and it was already a quarter to. Another match flared and I flushed the charred remnants of the postcard down the toilet. I sprinted back to the recording studio. Andi was toying with a cigarette.

'Have you seen my matches?'

I tossed the pack to him then told him I had to leave.

'What? Jakob, come on, man, help me get through this. Why?'

I hadn't really thought to plan an excuse. I improvised. Badly.

'My girlfriend's mother is ill. Very badly ill. She's – er – upset. My girlfriend, that is. Her mother is ... ill. As I said.'

He rubbed his eyes. 'Since when do you have a girlfriend? What's going on?'

'Sorry, I – I have to ...'

He said something else, but I was already heading out the door. No time to wait for the lift so I took the stairs two at a time, my bag bouncing against my back. Out on the street, a thin drizzle hung in the air. The tram stop was two blocks away – but I'd have to change lines to get to Café Bruno. Or, if I went a few blocks further I could get the metro, which might be quicker. I couldn't decide.

Instead, I ran.

HARRY

That evening, after sending my letter to Jakob, I sat eating my dinner as my mom stared out of the window. I tried to keep my voice calm as I told her we had a new science project at school and I would be leaving early on Friday morning to work on it. She didn't bat an eyelid, just nodded and smiled.

I spent the next few days gathering provisions and worrying whether I was doing the right thing. I stole a torch from the kitchen drawer and found a thin piece of rope near the bins at school. My plan was to use it to hold the trunk lid in place without the lock clicking and trapping me inside. I also left a note for Marie at Dieter's store, in case I missed our meeting. I didn't mention anything about Dad or the tunnel, or what I was about to do.

When Friday came, I had my alarm set for 4 a.m. It was under my pillow to muffle the sound, but I didn't need it. I didn't sleep at all that night. In the early hours of the morning, I thought about quitting – pretend none of this was happening. But I knew The Fly wouldn't quit just because things got risky. So when my digital alarm clicked round from 3:59 to 4:00, I leapt out of bed to start my mission.

I dressed quickly in the dark, then crept down the hallway to break into the study one last time. I took the map of Berlin from the desk and shoved it in my pocket.

Next, I took my dad's car keys, snuck out of the apartment and went down to the shared garage at the back of the building. I located my dad's BMW, unlocked the trunk, and left it slightly ajar as I went back inside to put back the keys in the study. I was pretty sure my father would be driving himself for this kind of trip. He'd never been comfortable being driven around and I doubted he'd want anyone knowing where he was going.

I paused outside my parents' bedroom door; I could almost hear them breathing. I wished I could kiss my mom goodbye. But I knew that if I was caught, I might never see her again.

I closed the study door and went back down to the car. I climbed into the trunk and took out the piece of rope. I fed it through a hook on the underside of the trunk and pulled it close on top of me. The trick was to make sure it didn't go all the way so that the lock didn't click, but the trunk still looked shut if anyone should glance at it.

I realised as I lay there that it was only the second time I had been in my dad's car in all the months we had been in Berlin. The first was when we had gone to visit Dieter's shop. I thought about the plans we had made back home. The drives around West Berlin we were going to take on weekends to get to know the place together, as a family. But none of it had ever happened. Instead, here I was, in his trunk, trying to find out what it was my dad was hiding from us.

I waited in that cramped, dark space for what felt like a very long time. There was a chance, of course, that he would find me in here. That, instead of throwing his briefcase and overnight bag on the back seat like he normally did, he'd decide to put them in the trunk.

The hours ticked slowly by. I doubted myself, over and over. Finally, I heard footsteps coming downstairs and the door to the garage open. Someone walked towards the car, but then kept going. I heard a car a little further along start up. I took several deep breaths and tried to stay calm as it drove away.

Five minutes later, someone else entered the garage.

This time the footsteps came straight over to the car and I heard the door unlock. I heard Dad throw his bags in the back and felt the slight movement as he settled into the front seat. I let out a sigh of relief as the engine started.

I rolled slightly against the back of the trunk as Dad drove out of the garage. This was it. I could scarcely believe I was doing it. If I was right, the world I would see when I got out of this car was the one I had only ever seen from my bedroom window. The other side of the Wall. The mysterious East.

I felt every bump in the road as we drove along. I hadn't considered how uncomfortable the trip would be. Even on smooth roads I was thrown around like a sack of potatoes and had to grip the rope tightly to prevent the trunk opening. I tried to stay silent, hoping Dad wouldn't notice anything strange with the balance of the car.

We seemed to get faster as we drove along and I was flung against the side of the trunk whenever we went round a corner. I lost concentration for a moment and the thin piece of rope holding the lid shut slipped from my grasp. I watched in horror as the trunk slowly started opening. The roar of the traffic grew louder. All it would take was for my dad to glance in his mirror and he'd see something was up and pull over to investigate. I made a grab for the rope but missed. Then I grabbed the trunk lid itself and pulled it downward. I could feel the wind on my knuckles as I tried to keep a grip. Suddenly, the car stopped and the lid fell on to my hand. I stifled a scream and reached for the rope again, hoping beyond hope that my dad hadn't noticed anything. I strained to hear if he was getting up from the front. He didn't move; we must have just stopped at a red light. Then, we were on our way again.

After what seemed like an age – but was probably only another five minutes – we came to a stop. Ahead of us, I could hear the thrum of another vehicle's engine and the mumbling of German voices as someone spoke to the driver inside. It took me a moment to realise what that meant. The voices were those of the border guards. We had arrived at Checkpoint Charlie.

My hands were sweating and I worried about losing my grip on the rope again. I tried to make out what the voices were saying, but they were too far away.

Would they search every vehicle at the crossing?

Surely they didn't think anyone would be foolhardy enough to actually sneak into the East. I remembered the laughter of the young German man with his girlfriend outside of the apartment building. *Don't tell me you're measuring out an escape into the East? That would be suicide, no*? I swallowed hard and tried to think of something else.

The car edged forwards.

The voices were closer now – two of them.

They sounded serious, but I couldn't understand what they were saying. My nails dug into my palm as I gripped, hard, on to the rope. I heard footsteps, as one of the men started moving around the car. I had been an idiot to believe they might let a car across the border without at least checking what was in the trunk. The footsteps stopped somewhere near the rear right wheel. I held my breath. From this distance, he could probably see that the trunk was slightly ajar, but I didn't dare pull it any further closed in case it made a noise. And then I heard my father's voice in fluent German. He knew the language of our hosts better than I realised. The tone was calm and it was followed by laughter from both of the guards, like friends or comrades sharing a joke. There was a soft crunch as the guard nearest me took a step back and then the car started up again and we drove on.

I couldn't believe it.

I had made it.

I was in the East.

JAKOB

Pedestrians glared at me as I swerved past, and more than one muttered something about 'young people' under their breath. I ignored them. I kept glancing at my wristwatch as I ran through the damp streets, dodging the traffic, my feet slapping against the wet pavement. I watched the hour hand slide past eleven and forced myself to increase my pace, though my heart was thumping against my ribcage. At the time, it felt like I was running for my life. It wasn't until later that I knew what that really felt like.

I made it to Café Bruno by ten past eleven. I had to pause for a minute, hands on my knees, taking great heaves of oxygen into my lungs. Then I gathered myself, wiped the sweat off my brow, and swung the doors open.

The café was mostly empty at this time on a Friday morning – the lull before the lunchtime rush. An older man in an old-fashioned cloth cap sat sipping a glass of beer at the counter. A trio of chattering students occupied one banquette. A serious-looking woman was studying her newspaper.

No sign of Harry. It didn't occur to me to that we had never actually met and I had no idea what he looked like; I was sure, somehow, that I would recognise him. I peered into the shadowy corners of the café to see if there was anyone I'd missed.

'Jakob?' said a voice from the table beside the door that I hadn't noticed was occupied.

Dana.

She was sitting with a girl I didn't recognise. About the same age as her, wearing green eyeshadow and a yellow-checked waistcoat. A pair of empty coffee cups were on the table in front of them.

'Hello,' I said, stupidly. Her companion looked from Dana to me and back again. A smirk formed on her lips and I felt the heat rising to my face.

'What are you doing here?' asked Dana. 'Shouldn't you be in school?'

I glanced at her friend again; I couldn't say anything in front of her.

'Well,' said the other girl, 'I'm finished, so I think I'll leave you two to it.' She kissed Dana goodbye and smiled at me as she left.

'Sit down,' Dana said, indicating the spot her friend had just left. 'What happened? You're panting.'

'Have you seen him?' I said urgently.

'Uhhhh, seen who? What's going on?'

I raised a finger to my lips in a warning to be quiet, then sat next to her on the banquette. Her perfume smelt sweet, I noticed.

'Harry,' I said.

'*Harry*? American Harry? Why would I have seen him?'

I explained to her about Harry's letter. Her face grew more and more concerned as I went on. After I'd finished, she stared silently at the table for a while. When she raised her eyes to mine they were deadly serious. 'Does he think this is a game? Does he not realise the danger he's in, the danger he's putting us all in?'

I didn't know what to say.

'He's coming, Dana. Here! We have to help him. Maybe – maybe it's lucky you're here too. My English is not so good after all.' I'd told her before about my scheme with my schoolmate Jürgen to get better grades, and she snorted with humour at the memory. In truth, my letters with Harry had probably done more to improve my English than anything I'd done at school.

'Of course I will help,' she said. 'You know that.' She

thought for a moment. 'You know, it actually might be useful having him here. He can tell us about the West, his apartment block, what we'll find at the other end of the ...' She didn't need to say the word. 'We'll wait together. I'll get us some more coffee. But, Jakob?'

'Yes?'

'*Try* to look a little more normal? You're sweating, your clothes are a mess, you're out of breath. Honestly, any Stasi officer walking in here would know in a second you were up to no good.'

I went to the bathroom to try to compose myself. When I returned, Dana had moved our things to a more private table near the back. We sat together in silence, sipping our coffee.

We didn't have to wait long, as it turned out. At twenty past, the door to Café Bruno opened.

HARRY

The car seemed to bump along even more violently as we raced through the East. I guessed because the road surfaces weren't as good on this side. It wasn't long before we slowed down and came to a stop again. I heard my father get out and lock his door. I was relieved to hear his footsteps fade away, thankful he didn't need anything from the trunk. I was beginning to feel proud of myself for the way my gamble was paying off. My best guess was that we had driven straight to the address in my father's notebook and that meant I should be within walking distance of Café Bruno.

I waited ten minutes to make sure Dad was really gone, then another five minutes to build up the courage to get out of the car. I shuffled around to look through the gap between the lid and the trunk. I was in some kind of car park. I could make out several rows of East German cars. They were boxier than the cars in the West and even the newer ones looked like they were built to an old design. As far as I could tell, there were no people nearby. I let the trunk open fully and clambered awkwardly out, hoping that no one would see me. I felt sick with nerves as I crouched down at the back of the car. I pulled the trunk lid down, careful not to click it into its lock because I knew I would have to get back in there later. It was my only hope of getting back to the West. I was suddenly struck by the enormity of what I had done. I had been so caught up in the plan that I hadn't really worried about how dangerous it might be for an American boy in East Berlin.

I took a deep breath and looked around me. My father had parked amongst a row of cars close to a line of trees without leaves and a sun-starved patch of grass. I poked my head up above the car and saw a guard with a rifle in an East German uniform.

I ducked down again and took a couple of deep breaths.

Keeping my body low, I moved between the parked cars, trying to make it to the street I could see so close beyond the verge.

I heard a siren and then a shout.

Heart pounding, I stopped dead in my tracks.

I sat with my back against the tyre of a car and closed my eyes and prayed the siren wasn't for me. It faded, and

I mustered the courage to move, crawling the length of the last car and peering over the trunk.

The guard was talking to a man in a suit. Both of their backs were to me, so I made a run for the trees. From there, I could casually join the sidewalk, like I was just another East Berliner out and about on a Friday morning.

I found a bench to sit down and steady myself, to calm my heart and get my bearings.

This was the kind of thing that The Fly would take in his stride, but it took me several deep breaths to steady my nerves.

I took my map of Berlin out of my pocket and tried not to look conspicuous as I worked out exactly where I was. I hadn't been sure what people would wear in the East. I'd worried that my clothes would make me stand out, so I'd picked an old T-shirt and trousers that I hoped would blend in. I also had on my big green coat, which was the only one that still fit me. I felt a bit foolish when I saw that the few people walking around were all wearing jeans, just like in the West.

I could almost have imagined I hadn't changed country at all, but subtle differences gave it away. There weren't any billboards or advertisements here, which felt strange to me. I don't know if it was that or the dark clouds overhead that made the whole place lack colour. The buildings all seemed a little run-down, except for the complex on the corner that was presumably the one my father was visiting. It was bigger than any of the others nearby, but there was no name, no sign. I hoped it was an international embassy of some kind – friendly to people like me. I hoped that somehow, my father's business there was honest.

This complex was huge, stretching for half a block and dominating everything around it. I looked at the street sign on the corner and marked my current position on the map. It looked like it should be a fairly straightforward route from here to Café Bruno. I tried to commit it to memory before closing the map and moving quickly on my way. I didn't want to draw attention to myself as an outsider by having to get the map out again on the way there.

I kept my head low and avoided making eye contact with anyone.

For a minute it was as if I couldn't remember how to walk properly.

How fast was normal?

I matched my pace to a man about six feet ahead of me and told myself, 'I'm just another East German kid, going about my day.' I repeated it in my head and tried to assume the role I had given myself, but I couldn't help thinking of how everyone in West Berlin seemed to know I was American, even before I opened my mouth. I was halfway along the road before I remembered the Rolling Stones patch on my coat sleeve. I hastily tore it off and cursed myself for not having thought of it before.

It felt odd making my way through East Berlin, being somewhere so familiar and yet so different. The street signs were different here, the writing more condensed. There were shops, but they were plain, presumably run by the state. Just as in the West, they were still clearing some of the old war-damaged buildings. Here, it looked as though the buildings were being replaced with large, concrete constructions. Keeping my head down, I also noticed that the streets seemed cleaner somehow. It was as if everything had been hosed down, sanitised, leaving no room for error or anything out of place.

Keeping my head down worked, until I accidentally bumped into an old man. He wore an overcoat and a hat and the cold look of someone who had seen a lot in their time. He frowned at me and said something I couldn't make out.

'*Entschuldigung*,' I muttered in apology, praying he

wouldn't pick up on my accent. He said something else and when I offered no reply, he started speaking louder, almost shouting in my face.

People in the street began to stop and stare. All I could think to do was run. I turned and sprinted back the way I'd come, almost crashing into a woman with a pram before darting down a narrow alley and stopping to catch my breath.

What was I doing? How had I expected to be able to get around here? This was a whole other country and I was lost within it.

I cursed the balloon I'd sent across the Wall.

But I couldn't let Jakob down, not when I'd come this far. No one seemed to be following me, so I took out the map, hands still shaking, and checked over my position. I was only three blocks away. I pulled my hood up and steeled myself to go on.

I had grown so used to the Wall, that it was almost reassuring to be in its shadow once again. Friedrichstraße was familiar in a funny sort of way, it was a street I had seen at a distance from my own bedroom window. I moved to one side to avoid a pair of *Vopos* guards, who glanced at me briefly as they passed. I was so close, but my mind was still spinning after the encounter with the old man. I imagined a gun-shot as I approached the café. I imagined Jakob falling out on to the street, blood spreading across the front of his shirt.

And then I saw it. The real sign to the café shone like a beacon, a splash of colour in an otherwise grey world. Café Bruno with that missing 'r', just as Jakob described it. Miraculously, I had arrived unscathed. I glanced back towards where I had seen the guards, but they were long gone. I took a deep breath and went through the door.

Jakob had told me all about Café Bruno, but it felt strange to find a place like this in East Berlin. A dimly lit café bar with a stage to one side. The kind of place you saw in a certain kind of film, when the hero talks to a glamorous woman while a jazz band plays in the background. I glanced around nervously, looking for Jakob. I had never seen a picture of him and we had never described our physical appearance in our letters, so I wasn't sure I would be able to spot him.

I needn't have worried. In the nearly empty café, we saw each other almost straightaway. He was sat in a booth near the back, staring at me as I walked in. I was surprised to see a girl with him, who turned to face me too. She looked like she belonged in cool cafés like this one. Jakob looked more like I felt, a little out of his depth.

'Harry Rogers?' she whispered as I got to their table.

I nodded, suddenly unable to speak.

'Please join us,' she said, 'and keep your voice *low*.'

I sat down and looked across at Jakob, who by now had both his hands on the table, fists clenched, biting his lip, eyes not moving from his coffee cup. He was dark haired and pale with dark green eyes. His clothes looked a little too small for him, as if he'd gone through a growth spurt recently and hadn't bothered to replace them.

The waiter came to take my order and before I could blink or even pretend to read a menu the girl was ordering a coffee for me. I had never drunk coffee before, but it seemed like the kind of drink you were supposed to order in a café like this.

I unzipped my coat and tried to relax.

'Hello, Jakob,' I whispered. He looked younger than I was expecting from his letters. I had expected someone cool, like the girl he was sat with. Instead, he looked skinny and scared like me.

He looked at me for the first time since I had sat down. He spoke in stuttering English.

'What ... are you doing here, Harry?'

'How the hell did you make it into the East?' said the girl.

I was taken aback. I'd expected Jakob to be as excited to meet me as I was to meet him.

I had been thinking about this meeting all week, but now that I was here, I didn't know what to say.

Jakob stared at me. He looked like he was trying to sort out the sentences in his head before saying them, and when he did speak, his speech was measured and careful.

'Harry, I know you came here with good intentions, and I'm glad to finally meet, but—'

'You should not have come here, Harry,' the girl said. 'It is dangerous for you. For us now also.'

I looked at her. 'I'm sorry, who are you?'

'I am Dana Decker,' she said, leaning in close so her whispers wouldn't travel. 'I am one of The Stamp Collectors.'

So this was Dana. Jakob had mentioned her in one or two of his letters, but I hadn't thought anything of it, I'd assumed she was just a friend of his. Meeting her in person, though, she seemed formidable.

'Well, Dana, there's something you don't know,' I said, a little unsure if I should continue. 'The exit point for the tunnel, my apartment building, is more dangerous than I'd originally thought. There is a spy there working for the Stasi.'

Dana stiffened at the mention of that word. 'Oh, come on,' she said, sounding disbelieving. 'How can you possibly know that?'

'Because I just hitched a lift over the border in the trunk of his car,' I said. 'Because he's my dad.'

A stunned silence fell upon the table. Jakob looked at me in disbelief. Nobody said anything for a second or two as the waiter returned with my coffee. I took a sip, and it had a strange bitter taste that I didn't much like.

'Christ,' whispered Dana. Then I spilled out the whole story. I told them about the things I had found in my dad's study. About the piano notes and the broadcasts, and the place he had driven to.

'Where was it?' asked Dana.

I pulled out my map and showed them where I had marked it.

Their faces went white. They looked at each other and then back at me.

'What?' I said. 'What is it?'

Dana's words were slow to form, as though she didn't want to tell me at all.

'Harry, that's ... that's Stasi HQ.'

It felt like a punch in the gut. Weeks of suspicion confirmed. Dad was involved with the Stasi, working for the East. He was a traitor and a spy and he had been lying to his family.

'So,' I said, my voice wavering, 'our fathers are working for the same side. Perhaps they might even know each other. Now wouldn't that be funny?'

Jakob spat out his reply.

'Hans is not my father,' he said, and then looked away from me. 'Sorry, I did not mean to snap.'

'This changes nothing,' Dana said. 'I am sorry and sad about your father, Harry, but the tunnelling will continue.'

She bombarded me with questions about the basement and the way out. She wanted to know if there were any empty apartments in my building, somewhere they might all be able to stay for a night or two until they had things figured out.

But I was still reeling from the confirmation my dad was a Stasi spy.

'You don't understand,' I said. 'My dad is powerful – dangerous even. If he finds you, or the tunnel, God only knows what will happen.'

I fixed my attention on Jakob.

'I don't know how much time we have,' I said, 'but the car will not sit there forever. I can get you out. That's why

I came here. The two of us will easily fit in that trunk and we'll be back in the West by morning. I can help you find your mother and sister. You can be with your real family.'

Jakob looked at Dana and Dana looked at me.

'Harry,' she said, in the tone of a kind teacher. 'You have been very brave. Thank you for everything you have done. But it is too risky for Jakob to go in the car. If they found him, they might kill him straightaway. You too, if you were caught. Alone, at least you can say it was a joke, a prank as you say. Maybe you will be safe. It sounds crazy, but the tunnel is the best way out for us.'

She said something in German to Jakob and he looked at me.

'Please, my friend,' he said. 'Dana and I know what we are doing. You do not know how bad it can be.'

I felt like crying. I was out of my depth and I just wanted to go home. I felt young and naïve next to the two of them, like their stupid younger brother. To them, I must have seemed like a fool. A stray dog in need of a pat on the head.

Jakob smiled at me.

'I will take you back to the car, Harry. I know a quick way.'

I nodded, stood, said goodbye to Dana. I wasn't sure

if the look she gave me was one of pity or disdain. But I could understand how she felt. Being in my presence alone jeopardised everything she had been working for.

My only hope now was to get home. To forget this and carry on with my life. To stop trying to play the superhero.

JAKOB

Outside Café Bruno, on the streets of Berlin, the thin crowd passing by seemed full of watching eyes.

'I thought people in the West would dress a little smarter than you,' I said, trying to look like we were just two regular teenagers chatting.

'Right,' Harry said. 'I mean, we do. Only, I wasn't sure what you guys would be wearing so I—' He gestured down at his worn-out clothes.

'Right, and you thought we didn't have hairbrushes either?'

That made him laugh. 'Give me a break,' he said. 'I just spent the morning in the trunk of a moving car.'

I hadn't wanted to admit it in front of Dana, because I knew what Harry had done was incredibly dangerous, but I was kind of proud that he'd managed to make it into the East. And I enjoyed talking to him as we made our way quickly though the city, heading towards Stasi HQ and his father's car. Now that the pressure was off and he knew I wasn't going to try and sneak out with him, he seemed to be enjoying seeing the other side of the Wall. He asked questions about the places we were passing and life here. But our small talk couldn't distract me entirely from worrying about what was around every corner.

I knew I was being paranoid, but I felt sure we would run into someone from school, who would introduce themselves to Harry and then realise that he couldn't speak German. Or that Margot would emerge from a shopfront, her pale blue eyes noticing my companion and immediately understanding my secret.

At one point, I was so sure I saw Hans that I pulled Harry into a side street. But when the man passed, I could see he looked nothing like Hans. He must have been six inches shorter and ten years younger – it was just that he had the same shade of brown hair.

After we had crossed the river, I led Harry down the narrower streets, avoiding the major thoroughfares. As we walked, he peered about, taking everything in, mesmerised by his surroundings.

I checked to make sure no one was within earshot. 'Is it very different to the West?' I asked.

'Yes ... No. I don't know. The buildings look similar, the

people. But it's not what I expected. I thought it would be like living in a prison. But it's not.'

It made me think about what life in the West would be like. On the one hand, everything we were told implied that the Western way of life was shallow and corrupt, but nobody really believed that. Instead, when we talked about it we assumed that it was a land of plenty – men in sharp suits and sunglasses chatting with beautiful women in bars. Everybody happy. Sunshine all the time.

But then, the weather couldn't really be all that different, and seeing Harry, who was not so different from me, made me wonder how wrong I might be about life on the other side of the Wall. What would I notice when I got across?

If I get across, I reminded myself.

I thought again about Harry's father's car, and his offer of returning with him to the West. On the one hand, it was risky. If we were found crossing the border, Harry might escape punishment and I would be imprisoned, or worse. And it would mean abandoning, even endangering, Dana and The Stamp Collectors. *And* I had told Dana that I would not go with Harry. *But*, I thought to myself, *if it does work, I could search for my family – perhaps even the government there might help me ...*

The streets opened up as we approached Stasi HQ.

The complex itself had nothing but its size to mark it out as special. Somehow, all its ordinariness only terrified me more. How could somewhere so normal contain an organisation that wanted to control all of our lives? I noticed a pair of guards pacing up and down, chatting. I could see the pistols in their belts from across the street.

'Keep your head down, keep quiet,' I whispered to Harry. 'People here know me.'

A line of cars stretched along the road in front of Stasi HQ. I tried hard not to turn my head and check on the guards as we walked past them. I decided to pretend that instead of housing the full might of the GDR's security service, it was just the government department for managing rubbish collection. It didn't help.

Harry stopped in front of an old car, a Trabant, made here in the East, with rust spreading like mould across its hub-caps.

'Here,' he said.

It didn't look like a diplomat's car, but, I reasoned, perhaps Harry's father wanted to remain incognito in the West.

And now the moment of decision was upon me – would I get in the trunk with Harry, or wait until the tunnel was finished? Even getting in the car was perilous, given how close we were to the Stasi building. But then I realised that, if no one found us, I could be in West Berlin by tomorrow. I would be one step closer to my mother.

'I'm coming with you,' I said.

I had my hand on the trunk when Harry spoke.

'No.'

'No?' I rounded on Harry, forgetting what I'd said about staying quiet. 'What do you mean?'

Harry's brow was creased with worry. 'This isn't Dad's car.'

'What?'

'This isn't my dad's car. It's gone.'

For a moment we just stood there, staring at each other. From the corner of my eye, I saw one of the guards in front of Stasi HQ look towards us, and I grabbed Harry's elbow and steered him quickly away.

'I was too late getting back,' said Harry. 'I'm stuck here.'

We were sitting on a park bench. An icy breeze shivered through the leaves above our heads. A toddler ran up to us and stared, head tilted on one side, before his mother silently collected him, glancing at us as if she knew we were guilty of something.

'Your father – you said he was supposed to be staying here overnight, right? Maybe we can still—'

'I wouldn't know where to start looking. Hell, he could be anywhere in East Berlin — anywhere in East Germany – by now.'

'Well, what if we just took you to the checkpoint?' I asked. 'They'd have to let you through, you're American.'

'I don't know,' he said. 'It looks pretty suspicious, doesn't it? An American boy turning up on the Soviet side of Checkpoint Charlie. They'd want to question me, that's for sure. And I don't mean border security.'

He was right. There was no way that the police wouldn't alert someone from the Stasi if we turned up like that. And if the Stasi started questioning him ... well, I trusted Harry, but the Stasi had their ways, and he knew a lot. We could all be in trouble.

What was I going to do? I was responsible for an illegal American, the son of a diplomat – apparently a spy – without papers, who could not pass for German.

As the afternoon wore on, I began to realise I was completely out of my depth. But Harry didn't panic. I was impressed by his courage. If he had got here all by himself, to help a stranger, then surely if we worked together, we could get back over the Wall. Both of us.

First things first. I needed to find somewhere for Harry to stay.

I thought of Dana. She lived alone, and there was a couch in her apartment for Harry to sleep on and she was, of course, completely trustworthy. But she had been in trouble with the Stasi so recently. And she already suspected the woman who lived across the landing, Frau Albert, of informing on her. No, Dana's wasn't safe.

'I might know someone who can help,' said Harry.

'What, here?' I was surprised that Harry seemed to be better connected than I was in my own half of the city.

'His name is Dieter. He's from the East, but he used to run a comic-book store in the West – that's how I know him. My dad got involved and got him sent back over here. Dieter still knows people in the East from before, though – I think he'd know what to do.'

But I had no idea how to find him and neither did Harry.

I briefly considered smuggling Harry into my room at the Eberhardts' apartment, but there was no way I could keep him concealed for long. Margot went into my room to clean at least once a week when I wasn't there.

Then it occurred to me. I knew where we could go.

I leapt to my feet and started to walk.

The outside of the building was meant to impress, to dazzle – the opposite of the worrying normality of Stasi

HQ. Even in the dullness of the day's weather, its metallic façade gleamed. A hundred polished windows reflected the occasional burst of purple sunset. I could tell Harry was impressed too.

'So this is the Funkhaus,' he said. I'd told him about it in our letters. 'But why are we here?'

'Trust me,' I told him. I didn't want to risk saying the plan out loud. Not because I was worried about being overheard, but because if Harry spotted any problems with it, we didn't have anything else to try.

That afternoon there was a concert being held at the Funkhaus. A crowd of smartly dressed men and women filtered through the revolving doors. I drew Harry with me, and we merged with the chattering crowd, eager for that evening's performance. They flowed up two flights of stairs, heading to one of the big concert halls. I pulled Harry down a deserted side corridor, hoping that no one would follow us or consider it out of the ordinary. I didn't dare look back to check if anyone had.

Before, the curving corridors and modern architecture of the Funkhaus had seemed beautiful and calming. Now I felt I was leading Harry through a dangerous gold-and-white maze of stairs, empty passageways, closed doors.

We headed up to the fifth floor. Here, I knew the

Funkhaus was much less busy. In my early weeks there, I'd spent a long time exploring its corridors and seeing where everything went. I knew that up here there were storage rooms, disused studios, rooms that had never even had a purpose. Hans' second office was up here somewhere too, which worried me. In all my time at the Funkhaus, I'd only ever seen Hans once, when he'd come to see the orchestra practise. But there was always a chance he might decide to make use of that office for something. I prayed that he and Harry would never come across each other.

I began to try doors. Most of them were locked, but finally one opened into a small studio, no bigger than a large cupboard. Big enough for what I had in mind. A naked light bulb dangled from the ceiling and, thankfully, when I pressed the switch, it flared into life. Someone had used this studio for storage – boxes of tapes and a stack of speakers were piled in one corner.

'Well?' I said to Harry, indicating the room.

'Here?' he said. At first, he looked perturbed. Then he nodded and laughed. 'Here!' He picked up one of the tapes and read the spine, an unreadable studio-engineer's scrawl. 'At least I'll have something to listen to.'

Someone had left a key in the back of the door. I tested it and it worked. Hopefully, this would give Harry some security, for a time at least. I wasn't sure how long he would need to stay. And there was nothing to sleep on. Nothing to eat. This really was like a prison.

'Just ... stay in the room,' I said. 'Keep the door locked, yes?'

Harry nodded. I was sure he understood the danger of him leaving. There was no way he could pass for a local, not with his poor German. And if he was discovered ... well, that would likely spell the end for all of us.

'I'll go and get some food, some ...' I wanted to say *blankets*, but I didn't know the word in English. 'Things,' I finished.

'Thank you,' he said, looking around nervously. 'I'm sorry for all of this.'

'No,' I said. 'It is I who should thank you. For reaching out. For trying to find my mother. From now on, we are doing this together.'

HARRY

After Jakob left, I felt deflated, exhausted. I kept an eye fixed on the door. The key was safely on my side of the lock, but I worried that would not be enough. Someone would sniff me out.

I thought about home. Mom would be missing me by now. What would she do? Would she go to the police? It broke my heart to think about her worrying, and I cursed myself for being so reckless. Even if everything had gone to plan, she would have had a night of stress and tears with no one to support her. And now, who knew when we'd see each other again? When Dad got back the search would really be on – whatever his motives were, I was sure my dad would be keen to find me.

In the stillness of the room, I realised how furious I was with him. I wanted to shake him. Wake him up from whatever craziness had led him to become a traitor. I should have confronted him. Pleaded with him to stop his work, the damage he was doing, to quit right away and get us all back to America.

Instead, here I was, stuck in this cell of a room, stuck in the East. I felt stupid for ever thinking I could be a hero like The Fly.

Hours later, the knock at the door, the rat-a-tat-tat I'd agreed with Jakob.

He had brought food. Dana was there too, with a blanket.

I took some bread and devoured it quickly. When I looked up and saw the two of them staring, I apologised.

'Sorry,' I said. 'I was starving.'

Dana smiled. She turned to Jakob and said, 'He is just like you.'

Jakob's reply was in German so I couldn't understand, but it made Dana laugh. 'He says he doesn't eat like that,' she translated, 'but I know the truth. I've seen him when he's really hungry.'

It was nice to experience a moment of calm, but there was no avoiding the situation. I think they could see my desperation for a way out. Dana spoke again, trying to sound reassuring.

'I'm sorry, Harry. I think you are going to have to

hide out here for a while, but we are going to help you in whatever way we can.'

'How do I get back home?' I could hear the crack in my voice.

Dana sighed. She looked at Jakob and then back at me.

'You will have to come through the tunnel with us.'

I got a sinking feeling in my gut. I had come here to try and warn them that the tunnel was too risky, and now, it was my only way out as well.

'I am sorry,' said Dana.

'There really is no other way?' I said.

'The Stasi have suspicions about The Stamp Collectors,' said Dana. 'I am certain I am being watched. We can't risk trying anything else. It is crazy, but the tunnel is our best way now.'

'How long?' I said. 'Before it's ready?'

'It is nearly finished. We are working harder, for longer. We think we are only days away.'

'You should see the work they're doing down there,' added Jakob. 'Believe me, I joined them for a shift and well – it's incredible.'

Dana took my hands in hers and said, 'Harry, I cannot tell you if we will make it or not, but we are close. So close. You have been very brave coming here. Don't worry, we will do everything we can to get you home.'

'You are our friend,' said Jakob. 'We won't abandon you.'

'Listen,' I said. 'I know someone who might be able to help. Or, at least, if you can find him, he deserves a way out of here. Dieter, Dieter Schulze.'

'Yes,' said Dana, 'Jakob told me about him. I don't know, Harry – if he was brought over to the East, well … we'll ask around, but it's dangerous. For him and for us.'

They left soon after, timing it so they could join the crowd leaving the concert hall after the performance.

Alone again, I took a final bite of food and put aside the rest for the morning.

I was so sure I would be discovered that I barely slept that night. An hour or so after Jakob and Dana left, I thought I saw the door handle move in a quick half-turn and back again. I stiffened in the corner. I heard footsteps walking away. I hoped it was some engineer or maybe a lost musician who'd now given up on the room, and not some officer gone to fetch a crowbar for the door. I waited for hours afterwards, straining to hear if they were coming back.

I needed to find something to distract myself.

There was an old mixing desk against one wall. Four

feet long with loads of dials and sound mixers. I imagined there was one in every room throughout the Funkhaus, recording the beautiful music. Something about that made me feel a little safer – the way that people enjoyed music, wherever in the world they were. Whichever side they were on.

I couldn't hear a thing through the walls of the sound-proofed rooms, but I imagined a group of East German musicians nearby, playing into the night.

I switched on the mixing desk. Tiny lights flickered and lit up. I turned the volume dial low and began trying switches. I pretended to be recording The Rolling Stones, with the lead singer, Mick Jagger, right there next to me, asking me for my advice.

I was messing around, turning dials and flicking switches at random, when my elbow hit a button at the bottom of the mixing desk. I could not believe what I heard. Somehow, I had managed to tune in to a broadcast, a piece of music played out over the airwaves.

It was unmistakable. The same kind of strange piano music that I had heard coming from my dad's office.

I felt a chill. The hair rose on the back on my neck, as if I was being watched. What did it mean? Was this the place where that strange music originated?

I turned off the mixing desk and sat back. I breathed slowly. I tried to stay calm and then it began to dawn on me. It was all meant to be – my ending up at the Funkhaus. I was never supposed to get back in my father's car. That wasn't my fate and I knew it now. It was like I had parachuted in behind enemy lines.

The mission was alive once more.

Jakob and Dana returned the next day with more food. Once the door was closed and locked, I told them about my discovery. I realised I must have been talking too quickly, because even Dana could not follow it all.

'Harry, please, it is hard for me,' she said. 'Slow down.'

'Okay, okay,' I said, and I sat down and repeated everything more slowly – about my father and the messages. About the transmitter in the study and about the piano notes he played. About the mixing desk and the broadcast.

'There are notes being passed. Messages in the music. They are sharing information. This must be how they get to have eyes and ears everywhere.'

Dana and Jakob looked at me like I was crazy.

'I have a plan,' I said. 'I know how the tunnel can be completed without the Stasi finding it.'

I wanted to make amends, to play my part.

'What're you talking about, Harry?'

'We break the code!' I said. 'Or, rather, I do. I have the notes I made at home; it was too risky to leave them lying around. And God knows I'll have enough time, being stuck here all day. With your help, I'm sure I can crack it.'

'And what would we do if we broke the code, Harry?' asked Dana.

'It's easy,' I said, standing up. 'We make a recording of our own and feed them false information. They know that something's going on, right? So we tell them we've found tunnelling, but tell them it's further along the Wall.'

Dana said something to Jakob in German and he nodded.

'I think maybe you are wrong, Harry,' Jakob said. 'This is just music, no? It is a bit strange, but it's just piano music.'

'No. Listen to me. I think I know how it works. The code, I mean. You have to trust me.'

Dana shook her head. 'I'm sorry, Harry, I know you want to help, but we have too many problems to waste time on your spy fantasies. Only yesterday, a friend of mine was nearly buried alive when a section of the tunnel collapsed.'

That made me pause.

'Is he OK?'

'Yes, yes, he's fine. It'll set us back a day, two at most.

They've already cleared the area and brought in more wooden struts to support the weakened section. But we have more than enough on our plates, Harry. We don't have time for your madcap schemes. I'm sorry.'

I looked at Jakob.

'Jakob? You must believe me.'

'Harry,' he said. 'This is not a game. This is real life. *Our* lives.'

'Exactly!' I said. '*Our* lives. My life too. And I need to get back to the West. Right now, that means making this tunnel plan work. You know how dangerous the Stasi are – we have to try anything that could help protect us.'

'Jakob,' said Dana, looking at her watch, 'we must go. We will be missed if we aren't at rehearsal.'

Dana left first and Jakob paused a moment at the door before turning back to me.

'I know I can do this,' I said.

He gave me the slightest of nods and then turned to follow Dana out.

JAKOB

Between school, my duties at the Funkhaus and The Stamp Collectors, I had a lot to cope with, even before Harry turned up. Now, with Harry hidden and work continuing on the tunnel, it became hard to keep on top of things. Sometimes, I'd forget where I was going or what I was supposed to be doing. I turned up for a mathematics lesson with a satchel full of sheet music. At orchestra, I opened my violin case and sent cornbread rolls meant for Harry scattering across the floor, to everyone but Dana's amusement.

While Dana did ask around about Dieter, she was careful not to mention why she wanted the information. There was nothing odd about this; people were used to information being shared on a need-to-know basis. We even managed to keep Harry secret from the rest of The Stamp Collectors. Why endanger them? Besides, grim as it was to think of, if they didn't know, they couldn't tell.

I didn't feel good about deceiving the band. They had become comrades, allies in the struggle – friends, in other words. During the week after Harry's arrival we practised twice, with another gig on the Sunday. I assumed that the gig was a cover for something going on with the tunnel – but I hadn't asked. It was safer not to know some things, especially with Hans on my case.

'Keep it together,' said Dana, after I'd hit a note so wildly off-key during rehearsal that the whole band ground to a halt. I had been worrying about Harry. Thinking about his theory on the musical codes. So it took me a second before I realised she was talking about the actual music. I expected the band to be annoyed with me for being distracted, but Ralf just shrugged and started up the beat again on the drums.

They had their own problems. Stress levels were going up as they got closer to finishing the tunnel and escape seemed to be an actual possibility. But at least they had homes to go to in the evening, somewhere they could relax. For me, home was the most dangerous place of all.

Not on the surface, of course. Since I'd agreed to inform for Hans, I was in favour again. The Eberhardts' apartment was all smiles and 'how-was-your-day' and jokes around the breakfast table. But whenever I came in from school or band rehearsal or the Funkhaus, Margot was there. Always in the middle of doing nothing, ready to come and help me with my coat, to bring me a cup of weak coffee.

After dinner with my adoptive parents a couple of days after Harry's arrival, I started clearing the dishes. To my surprise, Margot signalled that she would do it. Usually it was my chore, and today I wanted to do it. Dinner with Hans and Margot was a challenge. I had to stick to my story, remember the details about where I'd been, what I'd been doing. Hans would notice if I forgot exactly which piece we had been rehearsing at the Funkhaus, or who was at Café Bruno that evening.

Harry was excited about his plan to break the piano code. I wanted to help him, but my visits were always rushed. They had to be fitted into the gaps between my other activities so that the lies I told were as small as possible, leaving less room for mistakes. Standing in front of the sink, letting the hot water run over the plates and cutlery, was, if anything, a release from the pressure of keeping up my act.

But that night, Hans gave his famous smile and patted the back of my chair to indicate I should sit. Margot, after a long look at Hans, left us alone.

'Well, Jakob. You are certainly busy these days.'

It wasn't a question. He fixed his eyes on me and waited until I felt compelled to break the silence.

'Yes. I think my schoolwork is going well, though?'

Hans nodded. I detected disappointment. I knew what he wanted to talk to me about, and he knew that I knew. He would think more of me if I was the one to bring it up.

He said, 'Have you given any more thought to your future career?'

More stalling. But I had to go through with the act. It was all part of the game.

'Well, I have found that my interest in mathematics has been much greater, these last few weeks ... But still, though it is hard work, I think music is the right route for me.' Would it have been better to say that I had changed my mind, to give him exactly what he wanted? Or would that have been too obvious a lie? I could not tell. My life was filled with these tiny dilemmas.

'Well, of course music is a great Soviet pursuit. But I think perhaps you will change your mind one day.'

'Perhaps,' I said, thinking, *never*, never. A knot of hate for Hans tied itself in my stomach then.

I wasn't enjoying this little chat and I knew Hans would eventually steer things around to talking about Café Bruno, so I decided to cut to the chase.

'I have some information for you. From Café Bruno.'
Hans' eyes opened a millimetre wider. 'I ... I overheard
something.'

'Yes?'

'I think they are planning something. Something
about a secret printing press. Some anti-government
information – err, propaganda – that they want to spread.'
I had to tell Hans something. It was Harry's story about
Dieter that gave me the idea. The illegal printing presses
churning out copies of *The Fly*.

'Who?'

'Someone at the Café.'

Hans folded his hands together. 'Who?'

'... Gerold. Gerold Klug. The owner.' Forgive me, Gerold.
But I knew he was already in their files and hoped that
meant I was not putting him in further danger.

'Klug?' A muscle twitched in Hans' cheek. Was this
unexpected news to him? 'And who else? He must have
help – from the West, perhaps?'

'I – I don't know. I didn't see who he was talking to. I
don't think so.' Hans gave a tiny shake of his head. 'Sorry,'
I added.

'This isn't much, Jakob. One name. Some rumours. No
proof. I need more.'

'I'll find out. It's just ... I have to be careful. They are starting to trust me and I don't want to blow that.'

'Do whatever it takes, Jakob. Soon.' Hans was as cold then as I had ever seen him. A far cry from his attempts at fatherly kindness. This must be what it would be like to be one of his inferiors at work, or someone he interrogated.

Margot bustled in, dishes complete. She must have been able to tell something had passed between Hans and me, because she glanced over and smiled, trying to seem like she was on my side. I fled to my bedroom.

I lay on my bed, fully clothed. I knew Hans was growing suspicious. He'd probably already noticed differences between my story and what he was hearing from his other spies. My only hope was to get as far away from Hans as quickly as possible, so that he would have no chance of catching me or my friends. I had to do something.

Staring at the ceiling, I started to think about what Harry had suggested – the musical code, the fake signal. It seemed outlandish, crazy even, but I knew he was right. We needed an edge. I wasn't as sure as he was that we could crack it on our own, though. If he was right, I only knew one person who would have that information.

I started watching Hans more closely.

Paid attention to how he was dressed, what he carried

with him, what time he left the apartment, what time he got back.

He never worked at home, unlike Harry's father.

He didn't have an office I could go through when no one was in, and besides, Margot seemed to be in all the time.

He did carry a briefcase.

I rifled through it when he was in the bathroom. All it contained was a neatly folded copy of *Neues Deutschland*, a spare pair of reading glasses, a set of keys. He was too cautious to keep anything confidential there.

Where, then? Where, if I was Hans, would I keep these musical codes, if they existed? His office at Ruschestraße would be full of useful information, but the security there was too tight. I would never get in unobserved.

It struck me like a slap in the face. Hans' office at the Funkhaus! Sure, I'd never actually seen him in there, but where would be a better place for sending codes through the air waves? It had to be worth a look.

Getting to the door of Hans' office would be straightforward. I had proved with Harry I could get around the Funkhaus without being noticed. Getting into the room was another matter.

I went back to the briefcase and pulled out a set of keys. The keys for the room at the Funkhaus all had a similar design. I went through every key on the ring, but none of them looked right. My heart sank. As I replaced the keys in the case, I noticed something silver glinting beneath a confidential folder. I grabbed the loose key and held it up – it had to be the one! I shoved the key in my pocket and hurriedly closed the case, hoping to hell that Hans wouldn't notice. I'd make sure to return it as soon as I'd done what I needed to do.

I had practice at the Funkhaus that morning. I didn't want to draw anyone's attention to what I was doing – I wouldn't put it past Hans to have put one of his men on me – so I just went along to the orchestra and played my part. Dana and I ignored each other. We'd agreed, in order to allay suspicions, to not appear too friendly. I longed to go to her, tell her my plan – but perhaps there were some things it was better even she didn't know. After practice, as she left the rehearsal room, she lingered at the door. A brief smile, and then she was gone.

It was my turn to take Harry his food. I had two oranges and half a salami in my jacket pocket. But I was desperate to see what was in Hans' office. I ran up to the top floor of the Funkhaus, to the rarely used corridors. It felt like I had the place to myself, especially as it was a Saturday.

The only sound was the tapping of my footsteps on the hard linoleum floor. Once or twice, I got the feeling that someone was following me. But of course, when I turned round, no one was there.

The room number, 544, was etched into the key. There was no nameplate door, nothing to identify it. Just another anonymous office in a corridor lined with them.

To my delight, the key worked.

With a last glance down the empty corridor, I shut the door as quietly as I could behind me.

Inside, it was neat, free of dust. A desk. A filing cabinet. A large window. The sun struggled to break through the cloud, casting deep shadows.

Suddenly, I worried about leaving fingerprints. I hadn't thought to wear gloves. But it was too late; I was here. This might be my only chance, so I started to search.

I began with the filing cabinet. It was full of dusty manila folders, stiff light-brown envelopes containing reports on the movements of suspects. I flicked through a couple of them, but they just seemed to be full of boring detail.

Suspect Alpha left their flat at 7.00, bought a sandwich at 7.15.

Herr X entered the café at 10.05, sat and drank a coffee alone, exited 10.22.

I was amazed by how much there was of it, how many people seemed to be being followed every minute of the day. I had no idea why Hans would want this amount of detail, but then, the files didn't look like they'd been looked through in a while.

I moved on to the desk. It had three drawers. The top one contained pencils, all sharpened to fine points – Hans was nothing if not organised. The second drawer had three files marked 'Moderately Confidential'. Personal profiles. Possibly useful, but I didn't recognise any of the names. I replaced them.

The third drawer was locked with a combination lock. There were six dials with numbers around the edge from 1 to 9. I put my ear to it and tried twisting the dials, hoping I would hear them click into place, but it was a well-made lock and I couldn't hear any difference. I tried a couple of combinations that might mean something to Hans – his birthday, then Margot's – but nothing worked. I shook the drawer in frustration, rattling it loudly. That's when I remembered where I was and stopped. I strained my hearing, listening for footsteps, hoping the noise hadn't attracted any passing sound engineers to come and investigate. I forced myself to breathe slowly and tried one more combination: 070355. To my astonishment the lock clicked open. 7th March, 1955. My birthday.

I was shocked that Hans had chosen a combination that related to me. It reminded me that he saw me as someone important. I was his project, the boy he wanted to mould in his own image. I wasn't sure what would happen when he discovered I was not the person he believed I was.

In the drawer I finally discovered what I was looking for. A small book, not much larger than my hand. Written in neat ballpoint pen, it was filled with columns containing musical notes and letters of the alphabet, even some fragments of words. There was an unmarked cassette tape beside it too. I stared at them for a second, letting it sink in.

Harry was *right*.

I grabbed the book and the tape, ran out the door, barely remembering to lock it behind me, and sprinted down a floor to Harry's room.

HARRY

It was hard spending so much time alone. It gave me too much time to think. I would lie awake at night, thinking of my mom on the other side of Berlin. It must have been completely inexplicable to her, her only son just disappearing into thin air. It gave me a deeper appreciation of Jakob's quest to find his own mother. I would have given anything to be able to get in touch with her, to let her know everything was going to be OK.

Instead, I threw all my energy into trying to break the code. It wasn't going well. I had managed to tune in to the broadcasts a couple of times in the dead of night. I had even been able to work out enough of the mixing desk to record part of one of them, but I didn't know where to start decoding it. I pored over the notes I'd made from my father's book. I cursed myself for not paying close enough attention in German classes. I wished Jakob was around more to help. He was a proper musician who could read music well, not like me. Better still, he actually knew the language I was trying to decode. But he had his hands full, trying to maintain what looked like normality for his adoptive parents. I didn't think he had time to even think about code-breaking on top of everything else.

But then, on the afternoon of the fourth day, I heard Jakob's familiar rapid knock on the studio door, and he burst right in as I opened it.

I hadn't eaten that morning, so I was hoping he had brought some food. Instead, he was carrying a notebook and some kind of cassette tape. Without speaking, he went straight over and put the tape into the player.

A strange, staticky buzzing noise. It sounded like the white noise between FM radio stations. And then that familiar strange piano music. Jakob seemed to be listening intently. Once it finished, he rewound to the beginning, pressed play again.

'Might be an E?' Jakob said, stopping the tape after the first note.

Then he showed me the book. It was amazing seeing it all laid out like that. Here was everything I'd been straining to try and work out.

'Where did you get this?' I asked.

He looked up at me.

'Hans.'

And then I understood. I dug through the piles of equipment until I found the tuning fork I'd seen lying around. I struck the fork to get an A and we listened to the first note on the tape again.

'E flat,' I said, humming my way through the notes. 'Definitely, E flat.'

We both leant over the book. There were several E flats in Hans' early notes, but they appeared to refer to different letters. Perhaps there was more than one way of decoding an E flat? That would make sense – as I knew from my lessons, there are seven E flats on a piano. But which was *this* E flat? Did it depend on octave? Context? How long the note was held for? It didn't matter – I'd work it out. I had everything I needed now.

Jakob and I pored over the code book for a few minutes before he realised that he would be late getting home.

'Will you – do you think you'll be able to work this out?'

'Don't worry, Jakob, I have nothing but time. I'll work it out and then with all this equipment we'll be able to send out something of our own.'

'Good,' he said, almost to himself.

It was only as he was leaving that he said, 'Oh, I almost

forgot!' and pulled out a salami and two oranges from his pocket. I had forgotten how hungry I was, but eagerly grabbed at the first food I'd seen all day.

And then it struck me, the ridiculousness of it all. And I almost choked on a large bite of salami.

'Are you OK?' he asked, looking concerned.

'You know what this means, don't you?'

He shook his head.

'My father and your father. Walt and Hans. They know each other.'

There was something unnerving about the idea that my dad and Hans had been in contact like that. That they actually knew each other. It was disconcerting and yet somehow, it made Jakob and I more connected too. It was us versus them. It felt like we were brothers in arms.

I made good progress over the next couple of days. The code was kind of ingenious. Instead of each note always referring to the same letter, they in fact referred to a different letter each time they were played. Confusingly, vowels were often missed out entirely. I had to quiz Jakob on the potential German words different musical phrases might refer to whenever he came to bring me food.

Gradually, I worked through the message on the tape. I

felt like The Fly, breaking a code in order to trick the Stasi.

Snntg. 23:00 hr Chssnstrß. Agnt wrd bwffnt sn

The first section was easy to work out, even for someone still learning German. Sonntag meant Sunday, so there was obviously some kind of meet set. I figured that *Chssnstrß* might refer to a place and looking over my map again I was able to identify Chausseestraße, a street on this side of the Wall. *Agnt* I thought might refer to an agent of some sort, but I had to wait for Jakob to help with the final part of the message. He puzzled over it for a minute before looking up at me.

'*Agent wird bewaffnet sein,*' he said. 'Agent will be armed.'

I felt the air leave my body. Breaking the code had been exciting, fun almost. But this message was a chilling reminder of how serious the situation was, the danger we were in. Still, I wouldn't let it change my plan.

That afternoon, I worked through a recording I'd made of one of the other broadcasts. I had to check that the code didn't vary from message to message, double-check that it was always the code from this notebook that they used. Thankfully, I found another relatively straightforward message setting a meeting, this time on Tempelhofer Weg, over in the West. We were on the right track.

*

The following morning, when Jakob came by before rehearsal, I had my map of Berlin spread out on the floor. I showed him the location on the map I had identified as the spot we would say the tunnel was being dug. It was a café on Rosenthaler Platz, a couple of miles further up the Wall from Café Bruno. It was a risk of course but I was sure the distraction would give us an extra few hours at the vital time. I knew the notes, I'd written them carefully, and I knew the order to play them in.

Tnnlsgng, Cf Rnd, Rsnthlr Pltz

Tunnel exit, Café Rondo, Rosenthaler Platz.

I'd worked through the night and my brain was fried, but I'd never felt more alive.

'Harry,' said Jakob. 'I cannot believe you have done this.'

'There is only one problem,' I said.

'What? What is it?'

'We need a piano. That's the only way to use the code to record a message.'

He looked around the small room, as if there might be a piano hidden amongst the wires.

'Damn,' he said under his breath.

Suddenly, he became all action. 'OK, we can sort this. I have worked downstairs in one of the studios. There is a piano in there and a tape machine. We must go down there now. If anyone tries to talk to you, say nothing. I will do the talking.'

That short trip felt like a very long journey. I was terrified someone would question us as we made our way along the long Funkhaus corridor and down the flight of stairs. I tried to catch Jakob's eye, but he was focused on the task in hand. Two flights down and along a very long corridor, he pushed on the door of a studio numbered 33 and walked in without knocking.

There was a young man in there smoking a cigarette and finishing a recording of his own. Jakob said something to him quietly in German. The man spoke back, taking a long look at me.

I'm not sure what Jakob said next, but I definitely heard him mention his '*Vater*', which is the German for 'father'. Whatever he said, the man got up and left, brushing past me with a grunt as he went. Jakob locked the door.

I felt a rush of excitement. Finally, it felt like we were getting somewhere. I remembered that feeling I'd had hearing those eerily familiar piano notes on my first night in the Funkhaus, that feeling that there was a reason for me being here. Everything had led to this.

I sat down at the piano. I hoped Jakob didn't notice that my hands were shaking.

He was ready with the record button.

'Perhaps I'd better play it through a couple of times first,' I said, remembering my father's tentative playing.

'Yes, of course,' he said. 'But be quick – the less time we're up here, the better.'

I spread the page of notes on the stand and tentatively began playing through them. I wasn't any good at following sheet music, but I had spent so much time working out the message that I found I knew it almost by heart. After playing through the short passage twice, I looked up at Jakob.

'OK,' I said, 'I'm ready.'

He nodded and pushed down the button on the machine. I began to play. It was strange to think these simple notes would carry such significance. That they would call people to action. That someone, maybe even someone in this very building, would listen to them through headphones attached to machines attached to wires that spread out like an invisible spider's web.

I nodded at Jakob as I finished, and he stopped the tape. We both breathed out, two long sighs of relief.

'That's it, it's done,' I said.

Jakob looked at me and smiled.

'Thank you,' he said.

'You don't need to thank me. We're in this together, remember?'

His shoulders seemed to relax.

'Have you told Dana about all this yet?' I asked.

'Not yet, but I will. She won't say no. I will make sure of it.'

Jakob took the tape from the machine and gripped it.

'God, Harry, this might work,' he said.

'It *will* work,' I replied. 'It will keep the Stasi distracted, while we escape.'

'Now, I am afraid we must get you back upstairs,' he said. 'It will only be for a few more days.'

Back inside my abandoned studio he said goodbye.

'We will come for you,' he said. 'With a big push, Gerold thinks we should be ready by the end of the week. You have done great things for us, Harry. I am proud to call you an honorary Stamp Collector.'

JAKOB

I revealed what Harry and I had managed to achieve to Dana and Gerold that afternoon. The tape was sat before us on the kitchen table in Café Bruno, where Dana had first spread out the map of the tunnel. Behind us, a door led down to the basement where the tunnel was still being worked on beneath our feet. A route to the West and to freedom, upon which so much depended. I hoped it would all be worth it.

The tunnel was nearly finished. I knew Gerold was right that it was safer for each person to only know what they needed to know, but it made me appreciate how much we had to trust one another. When I told Dana about the plan that Harry and I had put in motion, she had only called on Gerold. It reminded me that we were not home and dry, not yet.

Gerold was not hard to convince. He did, in his gentle, harmless way, question the wisdom of telling the Stasi that a tunnel was being built. We explained that they already knew, or suspected, at least. And I knew that Hans had suspicions about Café Bruno.

'I saw your name on a file,' I told Gerold, 'in my father's office.' He received the news with the barest of chuckles.

'We need every edge we can get,' Dana continued. 'We're so close.' Gerold looked at us both, then nodded.

'Well, one thing is for sure, we can't broadcast the message from your wonderful Funkhaus, they'd trace that in a second. Wait here.'

He stood from the table and disappeared down the stairs to the basement. We could hear him moving about in one of the storerooms.

'Where is it, where is it … Aha!' A minute later, he arrived back with a dusty red suitcase. Inside was an ancient radio transmitter. The frequency dial and power switches were labelled in Cyrillic, the alphabet used for writing Russian. It looked like it hadn't been touched in years.

'Where on earth did you get this from?' Dana asked.

'During the war, some friends and I played at being Communists. For a time.'

I wondered out loud if it would work, but Gerold laughed and ran his fingers over the machine's still-shiny chrome.

'She'll work, don't you worry. This old girl's seen more scrapes than all of us put together.'

And, just as he promised, when he plugged the machine in, it whirred and clicked into life.

We needed to distract the Stasi at the best possible time. There would be no second chance. If the Stasi realised that their musical codes had been breached, their attention would be redoubled. If they traced the breach back to Hans, I would be a target too. So we decided to make the broadcast on Friday – the day the tunnel would be completed. We had a gig planned that evening to cover the sound of the tunnelling, although the tunnel itself was now so long that there was less danger of the noise giving us away. More importantly, it was a good excuse to get everyone together. All The Stamp Collectors, and everyone going with us, would gather for the crossing. The window of opportunity would be short. That was when we needed our enemies to be distracted. Dana wrote all the steps down, and we went over it again and again.

Friday.

I had forty-eight hours to keep up the appearance of my normal life. Luckily, the awareness of that sharpened my focus. Success or failure – either way, my life was about to change drastically.

HARRY

When Dana came to see me on the Thursday evening, she brought a rucksack with some bread and two apples with her. She lowered her voice to a whisper.

'Tomorrow, Harry. That is when we will go through the tunnel. Wait for me.'

'Did you – did you find Dieter? Is he coming?'

'I'm sorry, Harry.' Dana glanced down before looking directly into my eyes. 'We did and we didn't. I mean, you were right, he did come back into the East, but he hasn't been seen since.'

My heart sank. I don't know what I expected, but I couldn't bear to think about where Dieter might be.

'I mean, he might still be alive,' said Dana. I think she was trying to be reassuring, but if anything, it just made things worse. 'People do disappear and then turn up again. Not often, but ...' She saw the look on my face and stopped.

'Anyway, wait for me tomorrow. We are going to do this, you know. Thanks to your help.'

The clock on the wall counted the minutes. All I could do was hope that our plan would work. That the Stasi would be distracted by our false information long enough for us to escape. I tried not to think of all the things that could go wrong. To concentrate on everything working. On us making it back to the West.

I would explain everything to my mother when we got there. She'd get help for The Stamp Collectors, find them somewhere to stay. And we would contact the authorities in the American Sector and ask for protection from my father. I guessed they would put him on some kind of 'Wanted' list. I imagined him picked up at the checkpoint, handcuffed and bundled into the back of a car.

In West Berlin, The Stamp Collectors would breathe easy, no longer having to look over their shoulders. They would start new lives. They would play whatever music they wanted, without government interference. Maybe I'd even hear them on the radio one day.

We would find Ebba too, and Katrin. Maybe Marie had already found them. Jakob would move into his mother's modest apartment. Ebba would bake bread there on Sunday mornings and fill every corner with old songs from her violin. I pictured Jakob and Dana in cafés together, drinking coffee and chatting freely. Once everything was done, once they'd caught my father and extradited him back to the US, my mother and I would leave Berlin too. We would go back to D.C. or to her family in Philadelphia. Everyone would be OK.

These were the things I told myself while I sat and waited.

JAKOB

When Friday morning came, bitterly cold beneath a concrete sky, I went to school as usual for morning register, then found my friend Jürgen. I asked him to cover for me, tell the teachers or anyone else who asked that I had gone home sick.

He peered at me down his nose. 'What are you up to, old dog?'

I wished I could tell him. I wondered if he would want to come with us. I knew he had not bought into the lies being told by the people at the top of government, like our other schoolmates. And hadn't we been comrades too, in our small way, conspiring together against the system? But it was too late. I couldn't risk adding another person to the mission. So I just smiled and shrugged my shoulders and said, 'There's this girl ...'

He grinned. 'I'll cover for you.'

I never saw Jürgen again.

The first broadcast was set for midday. At Café Bruno, Gerold was out front tending to the patchy lunchtime crowd. They were all blissfully unaware of the tunnel nearing completion six metres beneath them. Dana and I sat in the kitchen by the transmitter and waited, looking at our watches every thirty seconds. Everything was prepared: the tape was connected, the frequency was set. There wasn't really anything to do either, we just had to press a couple of buttons and let the machine run. Still, my hands were trembling.

Five minutes to go ... three minutes ... two ... one ... thirty seconds ...

'Now.'

I pressed the button.

An otherworldly twittering filled the room, the piano notes that made no sense against the buzzing background of static. Dana and I, looking at each other over the kitchen table as our fake message floated off on the airwaves.

Dana shot to her feet.

'I – I should go. Ride uptown and see if they send anyone to investigate. See if they have taken the bait.'

'I'll come with you.'

'No,' she said, not meeting my eyes. 'Someone might recognise you. I'll be back for the second broadcast.'

And she was gone.

We'd planned the second broadcast for two hours later. I had nothing to do until then, so I went out front and offered Gerold a hand in the café. He set me to collecting crockery and wiping down tables. At some point, Cristopher arrived, the first of The Stamp Collectors. It was still a few hours until the show, and I was surprised to see him there early, but I thought he must have his own secret part to play. He followed me into the kitchen, glancing at the transmitter equipment laid out on the table.

'Hello,' he said, 'what's all this?'

'Oh, you know,' I said, 'just some of Gerold's old equipment. He was telling me and Dana about the war.'

'Funny, isn't it,' Cristopher said. 'We won the war, but Gerold still finds himself working as part of the Resistance.'

Later, after most of the lunch crowd had cleared out, Gerold and I were alone in the kitchen washing the dishes.

'Do you ever think about what you'll do in the West?' I said, more to distract myself from the tingling nerves in my head than anything else.

He smiled.

'Well,' he began, 'there are places I'd like to see in West Berlin. The Reichstag, the Tiergarten. I haven't been there for almost thirty years. And I'd like to travel more, if I can. Or maybe just get a job in a bakery somewhere, have my own place, without all this ...' He moved his hands about him, unable to find the words. But I knew what he meant. All this. The GDR, the state. Intruding, controlling. Watching.

His smile faded. 'And there's someone I want to see.'

'Family?'

'No. A woman I knew for a time during the war. We were close. But she made it over to the West before they put the Wall up. It is my deepest regret I didn't go with her.'

I had never suspected Gerold of having a romantic life. Though talking of it clearly pained him, his tone was matter of fact. Unsure of how to continue and not wanting to say the wrong thing, I murmured, 'Perhaps she has been waiting for you.'

Gerold snorted.

'Perhaps. Or perhaps she found someone else. Perhaps she has six children. It doesn't matter. I would just like to see her face, one more time.'

He finished drying a teacup, then turned his head to look at me.

'What?' I said.

'I'm not one to give advice. Never did like people telling

me what to do. And what does anybody know, after all, about life? We're all just lost in the dark, finding our way as best we can. But I will say one thing to you, Jakob. If you see a chance for happiness, don't let it pass you by.'

'What do you mean?' I said. But he just smiled, and said nothing further, and then I heard the doors to the café open.

It was Dana. She was breathless from the cycling, but she was grinning too. She ran over to me and grabbed my hands in hers.

'It worked. The plan. Well, your plan. Yours and Harry's.'

'It did?'

'It did. Further north, along the Wall, there are officers everywhere. They're trying to keep it a secret, but everyone can see, everyone's talking about it. Searching basements, going into people's houses. They fell for it. You did it.'

'We did it.'

She beamed at me. I looked down. I squeezed her hands tighter.

It was then that I felt someone's eyes on us. Cristopher. He looked a little annoyed. I let go of Dana's hands, feeling the heat rise in my face. Cristopher turned back to the paperback he was reading. Dana gave me a small nod, and together, we approached him.

'What are you two looking so happy about?' he asked.

We pulled up a couple of chairs and Dana quickly filled him in, outlining what would happen that evening. Despite our plan nearing completion, Cristopher didn't seem happy. I figured that perhaps he was nervous about finally going through with it.

'Sounds like you have everything in order, then,' he said. 'Nothing for me to do.'

'No,' I said, smiling awkwardly. 'I don't think there is anything—'

But Dana interrupted.

'What about Harry?' The plan had been that she would pick up Harry while I was at the Eberhardts', keeping up my pretence of a normal day. But I think she felt sorry for Cristopher, perhaps even guilty, though she had no reason to be, and she wanted to include him somehow. 'You could go and get Harry from the Funkhaus,' she said. 'It really would be a big help. And I'm sure Harry is ready to get out of that room by now.'

'Are you sure?' I asked Dana. 'Harry is expecting you, he doesn't know Cristopher.' I wasn't comfortable with the plan changing at this late point.

'No, it's OK,' said Cristopher, looking between the two of us. 'I can do it.'

HARRY

When the knock finally came, I rushed to the door of the room that had been my home for several days, butterflies in my stomach, saying to myself, *This is it, this is our time.*

But the door swung open with force and a pair of hands shoved me. A boot lashed out and kicked me in the shin. I fell backwards, tripped, and landed on the floor. When I looked up, two men were standing over me. One older, perhaps my father's age, and the other in his early twenties.

The younger man sneered.

'They said you would be here.'

The other man stepped forward. He was taller and wore a pristine suit with the badge of the GDR on one of the lapels.

He knelt beside me and smiled, while the younger man locked the door.

'Do you know who I am?' he asked. His English was

perfect. 'I am Hans Eberhardt, and you are in a great deal of trouble.'

Jakob's adopted father put his hand on my head and scrunched my hair in his fist. It might almost have been a loving gesture – the way a dad ruffles the hair of his child. Then he tightened his grip and pulled my head forcefully toward him, so he could speak directly into my ear. 'We know your game,' he said. 'You are not going to win.'

He lifted me to my feet, grabbed me under the arms, and shoved me on to a stool. He paced slowly in front of me.

'Thanks to Cristopher here, we have got to you just in time. It's incredible that you thought you might've got away with this.'

Cristopher? So that's how Hans had found me. This must be Cristopher Zweig, Jakob and Dana had mentioned him. I felt sick. The Stamp Collectors had an informant in their ranks.

Hans stopped, placed his hands on my knees and edged his face inches from mine.

My mouth was dry. I tried to gulp, to swallow. I could feel the fear rising inside me, the cold sweat at the back of my neck. I gathered what little confidence remained. I had come too far not to put up a fight. I had nothing left to lose.

'You cannot treat me like this. I'm an American.'

But my words sounded feeble and Hans just smirked.

'You Americans are all the same,' he said. 'You think you own the world. But at what price? I *am* the Stasi. You cannot get the better of me. It is impossible.'

Hans noticed the bag in the corner of the room. From the look on his face, I could tell he recognised it as belonging to Jakob.

I couldn't be sure what Cristopher had told him, but I had to assume he knew everything. Seeing Jakob's bag there was the proof of his son's betrayal.

Hans' manner changed again. He walked back towards me, towering over me as I lay on the floor. I tried to protect my head with my arms, as he took a swing at me. I was dizzy. I had a headache like I'd never felt before.

Hans stepped back. Cristopher, who had simply stood by and watched it all, handed Hans a cloth which he used to wipe the blood from his hand. I realised my nose was bleeding.

On the mixing desk, Hans noticed the code book that Jakob had stolen from his office. He leafed through it and flung it against the wall.

He turned back to me and said, 'There are many things we can do to you to find out what else you know, what else you have been involved in. You should never have come here, American pig.'

Hans instructed Cristopher to sit me back on the stool and tie my hands behind my back with old leads and wires they found bundled in a box by the wall.

'Well done, Cristopher,' said Hans, addressing him in English as if to make a point to me. 'You have done extremely well. You have shown that you are loyal. Like Jakob should have been. There is a place for you in the Stasi. I shall see that we make it official.'

They dragged me up and marched me out of the room and down the corridor. The sight of a bound and bloodied boy might have seemed alarming to the one or two people we passed, but one look at Hans forced them to nod and quickly look away. I might have appealed for help, told someone how I had just been treated, but I realised it would be a waste of time.

Even if they wanted to help, they would never dare.

I was taken up a floor to an office that I assumed was Hans', though it had no name on the door. Cristopher shoved me into a chair in the corner.

'It is fortunate all the rooms in the Funkhaus, even this one, are soundproof,' said Hans. 'No one will hear you.'

I opened my mouth to say something, but then shut it

again. Was Hans aware of who my dad was? Did it matter? I realised I wasn't even sure my dad would step in to help me – he was working with the Stasi now.

Hans turned and gave his parting instruction to Cristopher.

'Do not touch this boy,' he said. 'I want him for myself when I return.'

Cristopher hadn't moved for more than five minutes. He stood in front of the door with his arms crossed, playing henchman.

The silence between us was deafening.

All I could manage was, 'Cristopher? Cristopher Zweig?'

He looked down at his shoes, unable to look me in the eye. 'Yes, that's me.'

Maybe it was still possible to appeal to him.

'Cristopher,' I said. 'Come on, let me go. Please. We are Stamp Collectors, you and I.'

'I was never a Stamp Collector and I never will be,' he snapped.

'You were going to betray them all along? Dana? Jakob?'

'My love for the GDR is greater than any friendship. It is greater than music. The Stamp Collectors will be made examples of. All of them. But you – you are a prize we were not expecting.'

He spoke like it was rehearsed, like he was still trying his new position on for size; the Stasi's newest recruit was maybe lacking the conviction behind his brainwashed words. I sat and tried to imagine that I could overcome him somehow. That maybe this wasn't the end.

I gathered my thoughts and did my best to ignore my fear. I had to act rationally.

I looked around the room for anything that might help. Were there any loose vents in the ceiling? How high were we – maybe I could get out through the window? I glanced back at Cristopher and noticed that the key was in the lock on our side of the door behind him. All I had to do was get my hands free and wrestle past Cristopher. For a moment I doubted myself; I wasn't The Fly. But there was nothing to lose, and perhaps I had one last trick to play. I just needed to convince Cristopher to untie me.

JAKOB

I couldn't shake the feeling of unease that afternoon as I made my way home from Café Bruno. But, as I approached the Eberhardts', I felt a strange new sensation. It was the realisation that this was the last time I would ever see this place. The last time I would ever enter their apartment. I thought of its rooms – the small kitchen, the hallway with the long rug down the middle, the dustless living room with everything in its place. I had trained myself, over the years, never to think of the apartment as 'home'. But, as I pushed through the door to the building, and started climbing the granite steps that wound up the centre of the block, I wondered who I was kidding. It *had* been my home.

'Hello,' I called as I entered the apartment, injecting a note of breeziness into my voice.

From the kitchen, Margot called a greeting back and her head appeared around the door. She checked me over and smiled.

'Are you well, Jakob?'

'Very well, Mother.'

Satisfied, she vanished back into the kitchen.

I went to my room. It was all exactly as I had left it – the violin case propped against the wardrobe, the folded metal music stand beside it, my desk with my pile of textbooks in one corner. It was strange – despite how much I hated my adoptive parents, this room had been a sanctuary of sorts. A place I could go to be alone.

But there was no time for regrets. Tonight was the night.

I shook my head to clear it and turned my attention to packing. Warm clothes seemed sensible. My violin was needed as well, for we still had a gig to play. I folded up a couple of sweaters, a pair of trousers, two sets of underwear. My backpack was only small and that was all I could fit in without overfilling it.

Across the room, I noticed my records propped against the wall in an alcove. I would not be able to take them with me – not even one. They were an unnecessary burden. Yet, checking my watch, I realised I had a few minutes left before I needed to leave. I decided to put one on. To give my favourite jazz record, Duke Ellington, one last listen.

Some minutes later, I heard the door to the apartment open and the unmistakable click of Hans' shoes on the floor. Instinctively, I reached out and turned the volume right down. I listened as he went into the kitchen and said something to Margot, his words just below the level where I could make them out. Sitting up, I reached across the bed for my rucksack and began to fasten its buckles.

Click-click-click-click.

A sound I knew too well. I felt a tremor of fear.

He opened the door and took in the scene. One of his eyes twitched – an odd tic I hadn't seen before.

'Going somewhere?' he said. The rucksack and violin case were behind me on the bed.

'Yes,' I said, trying to appear calm. 'Café Bruno. I have a show.' I smiled at him. 'Is it cold out?'

'Very,' replied Hans. He stood in the doorway, silhouetted by the hall light behind him. He wasn't smiling, but that wasn't unusual. But when I broke eye contact to return to fixing my laces, I noticed something. From the sleeves of his suit jacket, white cuffs emerged – and on the right cuff were tiny crimson spatters. Blood. He saw me notice it, and then he spoke.

'I know it was you who took the code book.'

A deep pit opened inside me. 'What's that, Father?'

'Father?' he repeated back at me, heavy with sarcasm. 'Come, Jakob. Don't you think the time for lies has passed?

You got the key from my bag. You went to my office in the Funkhaus. You took the code book.'

What could I say? Every kind of excuse, every rationale for my behaviour flitted through my brain, none of them good enough. Hans was right. The time for lies had passed.

Hans continued, 'Your craft was good, Jakob. Replacing the key after you had used it. Very clever. In a way, I'm proud of you. I've always known you had potential. What a shame you had to waste it.'

I was still sitting on the edge of my bed. Hans stepped towards me, raising his hand as if to strike. I grabbed my violin case and held it as a shield in front of my face, but Hans ripped it from me and tossed it across the room. It hit the wardrobe and clattered to the floor.

Then the back of his hand struck me. I felt a warm sting on my face and tried to scramble back across the bed, but he kept landing blows all over my body.

'I failed,' he said, 'I failed, I failed.'

It didn't even occur to me to hit him back. It all happened so quickly.

'Hans – stop!' screamed Margot. I was so dazed from the rain of blows I hadn't noticed her come in. Somehow, she forced herself between me and Hans. She grabbed his wrists and managed to pull his hands from me. I slumped back on the bed and tasted blood.

Hans turned to face Margot. She held him still. Her hands looked tiny in comparison to his. He held her gaze.

'Get out,' he said. His voice was barely above a whisper. She backed away and out of the room.

'I know about everything,' he said, turning to me on the bed. 'About your little engineering project in the basement of Café Bruno. About the real reason for all those band rehearsals and about the American boy you've been working with.' I was in shock, I had always feared what would happen if Hans discovered what was going on, and here he was, stood in front of me telling me the game was up.

'I am so ashamed, Jakob. Not of you, not really. Of myself. I thought I saw something in you. The potential to be a good socialist. I thought perhaps I might mould you into something better than that traitorous father of yours. But I have failed. You have too much of him in you, I can see that now.'

Then he started walking up and down the room, flexing his fingers and muttering words to himself as if I wasn't even there.

'First things first,' he said. He held trembling fingers out in front of him and counted out his tasks. 'One – deal with this tunnel. Two – the American boy. You' – he turned to look at me, disgusted – 'I will save for last.'

I lay on the bed, stunned. I tried to move a little, but a stabbing sensation in my chest stopped me. I was bruised all over. It felt easiest, safest, to keep as still as possible. I could feel myself drifting into unconsciousness and I welcomed it. I wanted to be free from this apartment, free from the knowledge that I too had failed. That the plan was finished.

But, before I could let myself drift away, something flickered in my mind.

Something Hans had said.

'One – deal with this tunnel. Two – the American boy.'

I willed my brain to focus. Why would he have to deal with the American boy? Surely Harry was in the custody of the Stasi? Hans himself would never be involved in the imprisonment. He would have underlings for that, unless …

Unless the Stasi didn't know the full story.

I forced myself to stay alert; I had to think it through.

What would happen if the Stasi did have Harry, if they interrogated him? Of course, my name would come up when they asked him about his accomplices. No matter how brave he was, the Stasi had ways. And if my name came up, so would Hans'. How would that look, for him? No matter his rank, the fact that his own adoptive son had worked against the state would endanger his career – maybe even his freedom.

And Hans had failed. He had told me he had failed.

That meant Harry was not with the Stasi. Hans must have him somewhere else. And surely, *surely* there was only one place he could be.

I began to unfold my body. Every muscle ached. I was sure he had cracked a rib. I began to test my limbs, checked myself for broken bones. Pain shot through me in bursts, but I decided I would ignore it. No, not ignore it – I would use it.

I got to my feet and tried the door handle, even though I'd heard Hans lock it. It didn't budge, so I stepped back and prepared to smash it, one shoulder down – on the side away from my injured rib. But before I charged the door, I thought again. I listened. There was the faintest sound of sobbing, just outside my room.

I bent my mouth to the keyhole and said, in as pathetic a voice as I could manage, 'Mum?'

The sobbing stopped.

'J–J–Jakob? Oh, Jakob, Jakob. I'm sorry, Jakob, so sorry.'

'Mum,' I whispered. 'Please help me.'

She hurried to unlock the door. Seeing me, she brought her hand to her mouth in shock. My face must have been bruised, and I could feel one eye swelling.

'Oh, Jakob,' she said. 'Let me help you. Go back to your bed. I will bring a damp cloth. Poor, sweet Jakob.'

I didn't move.

'Please,' she said. 'Please, Jakob. Do as I ask. I will make sure he doesn't hurt you again. He should never have done this. I will leave him. We will leave him, I promise. Only, for now, go back to your bed. I will look after you. Please.'

She was in my way.

'I need to go,' I said. 'There is something I have to do.'

Tears ran down her cheek, messing up her make-up.

'No, no.' She shook her head.

She was not a large woman – perhaps one metre fifty. I had been taller than her since I was twelve. Even with my injuries, I was sure I could overpower her if I needed too. I thought of all the times that Hans had scolded me, told me I wasn't good enough, sent me to bed without supper for the tiniest wrong-doings. And how she had always been there afterwards to check I was OK, promising she would speak to him for me. A part of me wanted to just push her out of the way, but I couldn't do it.

'If you love me,' I said, 'let me pass.'

I could see in her face the battle that was raging. She loved Hans, it was true, but she loved me too – perhaps more. And I was forcing her to decide between us.

She stepped to one side.

I stumbled past her, towards the door to the apartment, rucksack and violin forgotten. I turned back as I reached the doorway, to see her standing alone.

'Goodbye,' I said.

HARRY

Cristopher yawned and looked at his watch.

'You should never have come here,' he said. 'Now you'll never see the bright lights of the West again.'

I shook my head in disgust.

I could tell he was pleased with himself, for the part he had played. The sneer on his face said it all.

'You're pretty comfortable there, aren't you?' I said. 'But tell me, what's it like being a puppet for a corrupt system?'

'You know nothing,' he said. 'You can never understand what we are trying to do here. You're just a child.'

'And you're a fool for thinking I won't find a way out.'

Even with my hands tied behind my back and everything looking bleak, I still had to believe I would escape.

Cristopher's manner changed. He stood upright and walked towards me. He wanted to hurt me. I could see it in him. Was it my defiance he hated? Did it remind him of something he was missing? I guessed being a soldier hadn't come easy to him. Perhaps there was still a conscience in there somewhere. There was a flicker in his eyes. To strike or not to strike. A way to prove to himself that he was fit for a career in the Stasi.

'Go on,' I said, trying to keep my voice calm. 'Do it. We'll see what Hans says when he comes back and sees fresh blood on me. After he told you not to touch me.'

Cristopher stalled and stepped back.

I told myself I would try one last time to appeal to his good side. One last chance. There must have been something there that Jakob, Dana and the rest of The Stamp Collectors had seen.

'Come on, Cristopher,' I said. 'What about the music you played? Jakob wrote and told me all about it. The accordion, right? Jakob told me about how the music brought you together. Like a proper band. A gang. We're the same, you and I. We are comrades, Cristopher. And I just want to go home. That's all I want. Please.'

My voice cracked at the end. I wasn't acting, I was scared. I wished my mother was near me, imagined my father swooping in and stopping it all, telling me I had it wrong all along.

Cristopher just laughed.

'Begging like a dog,' he said. 'This is funny for me.'

The past few weeks ran through my mind. How I had got there. My father. The messages. The car. The secrets. I was determined that none of it would be in vain. We had to make it to the West.

I spat, hitting him just beneath his right eye.

He stared at me for a moment, disbelieving. Then he wiped away my spit and took a swing at me, knocking me sprawling across the floor, chair and all.

'That was a big mistake,' he said. 'What do you think you're doing?'

I was channelling The Fly. Trying something daring, even if it made things worse.

'Sure, it takes a big man to punch a child with his hands tied behind his back.'

I had seen The Fly pull the same trick to get himself out of a jam with a gang of smugglers: goading them into releasing him, to make it a fair fight. I pictured the comic strip as I did it – the clearly drawn lines, the depth of colour and detail, the drama in each frame. It had seemed crazy, him taking on five men like that. But, at least untied he had stood a chance.

The odds weren't in my favour either. Cristopher was half a foot taller than me, and quite a lot bigger. If I was honest with myself, I didn't really even know how to fight.

'Why don't you untie me and see what happens?' I asked. 'Or are you worried you can't take an *Amerikaner* in a fair fight?'

I couldn't see him from my position on the floor, but I could hear his footsteps as he walked slowly towards me. I began to doubt myself; maybe his pride wouldn't stop him beating me up while I was defenceless. He crouched down behind me, close enough that I could hear him breathing.

'So, you want a fair fight,' he said. 'I think we can make that happen.'

I heard a ripping noise and felt the cables tying my hands together release, as if they'd been cut. The thought – *he has a knife* – flashed through my mind, but that didn't change anything. As soon as I was free, I rolled to the side and jumped to my feet. Then I dived at him, taking him by surprise, and we both went sprawling on to the floor. Quick as a flash, I was back on my feet and made it across the room to the door. I wasn't The Fly – I knew I was unlikely to win in a fight against Cristopher; my only real chance was to get away. I scrabbled with the lock and threw the door open just as I felt a hand grab my shoulder. Cristopher spun me round and shoved me hard and I fell against a rack of shelves.

I expected him to come at me then, but instead he stood calmly in the doorway. I watched as he reached slowly behind his back and drew out a gun. It had been tucked into the back of his waistband all along.

'My father's Luger,' he said, smiling at my surprise. 'He was a lieutenant in the German army during the war. A crack shot, apparently, before he died. I'm sure you won't be the first American to see this particular weapon. Hans will understand I had no choice.'

I knew the game was up. I closed my eyes and waited.

JAKOB

I fled down the stairs and out of the house as quickly as I could, almost tripping as I fell through the front door. On the street outside, I passed a couple of pensioners who smiled a greeting that turned to suspicion when they saw how awkwardly I was moving. I wondered what they must have thought of me limping down the street. Did they know whose house I had just left?

I didn't have time to worry about that now. My friends were in trouble and they didn't even know it yet. I pushed on to the corner, where there was a pay phone. As the adrenaline wore off, my bruises began to pulse. I could still taste blood in my mouth.

I started dialling before I realised that I didn't have a coin.

I rushed back past the house, to where the two pensioners were still making their way along the street. I could see fear in their eyes as I shouted to them.

'Hello! Hello! Please, I need change. You have to help me. For the phone, I just need some change.'

The man scrabbled in his pocket and thrust a couple of marks into my hand. I ran to the payphone without even thanking him.

Out of breath, I dialled Café Bruno. It rang and rang. I could imagine the phone sitting where it always sat on the end of the bar as everyone was busily setting things up. 'Come on,' I said angrily into the air, 'pick up.'

Nothing.

I hung up and tried again. Hans had a head start on me, and a car – what if I was too late? What if he was already there?

Still no answer.

I threw the phone receiver down in frustration.

I felt like I needed to divide myself in two. One to try and get to Café Bruno and warn everybody, and the other to try and find a way to help Harry. Time was running out – what could I do?

Outside the phone booth, a black bicycle leaned against the railings of the Eberhardts' apartment block. Someone visiting a friend, probably. Muttering an apology to the owner, I snatched the bike, swung my leg over and pedalled hard.

HARRY

I could hear my heart beating. This was it. I waited for the shot, but none came. I sensed a change in the light through my closed eyes, the beam from the corridor bulbs. I dared myself to look. I could see him behind Cristopher, creeping in with a finger over his mouth.

Jakob.

He stepped into the room and reached for a heavy music stand that was leaning by the door. He took a swing and hit Cristopher across the back of the neck.

Cristopher yelped and lurched forwards before turning and pointing the gun at Jakob. I got up from the floor and jumped onto Cristopher's back. He dropped the gun as he tried to throw me off, and we both fell to the ground.

Jakob's second swing of the music stand knocked Cristopher out cold. He slumped on top of me. I pushed him off and sat up, leaning against the wall and breathing heavily. Jakob dropped down next to me. I knew I'd never be able to explain how relieved I was to see him.

'Are you OK?' he asked.

'Just about. How about you?'

'Fine.'

'How did you get those?' I asked, pointing to the bruises on his face.

'Hans,' he said. 'You?'

'Same.'

'Monster,' spat Jakob.

'How did you know I would be up here?'

'I didn't think he would take you out of the Funkhaus – he's trying to keep all this under wraps. When I saw your room was empty, the first thing I thought of was his office. Where else could he hide you?'

Jakob looked across at Cristopher, unconscious in the corner.

'I don't know who to trust any more,' he said.

'Well, you can trust me.'

Then Jakob told me all about what had happened at his home. How Hans had somehow uncovered everything.

'What about the rest of The Stamp Collectors?' I asked. 'Are they safe?'

He looked down at his hands.

'I don't know,' he said. 'I came here first for you.'

'You chose *me* over The Stamp Collectors? Over Dana? Why?'

Jakob stood up. He looked down at me.

'I need you, Harry, I can't take on Hans on my own.'

He held out his hand to help me up.

'What are we going to do?' I asked.

'We have no choice,' said Jakob. 'The tunnel is our only way.'

'But, surely if Hans knows, there's no way.'

'Maybe, but he can't involve a lot of people without it coming back to him. I'm still his son as far as his colleagues are concerned. He'll have to deal with this himself, and that means we might still have a chance.'

JAKOB

We flew through East Berlin on stolen bicycles. Barely aware of the bruises Hans had given me, I pushed hard on the pedals, racing towards Café Bruno. The cool night air rushed past. Harry followed close behind. Dozens of sirens wailed in the distance. Perhaps that was why the streets were so quiet. That many sirens meant trouble, and who in East Berlin wanted more trouble?

From the Funkhaus to Café Bruno took all of ten minutes. The streets around the café were even quieter – deserted. We were close to the Wall, and though I couldn't see it, I could feel it. It was just around the corner, a threatening presence.

Café Bruno was dark and silent. There should have been lights. There should have been music, the clink of glasses and Gerold's belly laugh rising above the sound of the crowd. I just hoped the quiet meant that the rest of The Stamp Collectors had already made it through the tunnel somehow. I couldn't let myself admit how unlikely that was.

Discarding our bikes, we walked up to the windows and peered through. The café was a wreck. Splintered glass, broken chairs, ripped leather banquettes. The mirrored pane behind the counter had been shattered, shards missing like pieces of a sharp-edged jigsaw puzzle. Nothing moved.

'Wait,' Harry said. 'We don't know what we're going to find.' But I ignored him and pushed through the swing doors.

Inside, it was quieter still. A deadly silence broken by the occasional muffled siren and the crunch of our feet on the broken glass. It was dark too, illuminated only by the streetlights outside. I looked around the ruined café for a sign. The instruments of The Stamp Collectors stood on the stage, as if waiting for the band to emerge and start playing them, except Ralf's bass drum had a hole torn right through the skin.

The band weren't about to emerge. I knew it then. Hans had already been and gone. The Stamp Collectors had been caught: Ralf, Nadine, Viktor. And Gerold. Others too, friends of friends, people from the scene I recognised but whose names I did not know.

Dana.

All of them. They had probably been taken to anonymous concrete cells.

'We're done,' I said to Harry, collapsing into a chair. 'We're finished. I should just go straight to Ruschestraße and hand myself in.'

Harry paced around the bar, shaking his head, muttering in English, 'It's not right, it's not right.'

'Welcome to the GDR.' I put my head down on the sticky table and thought about everything we had lost, how we had failed. It wasn't right. But what did that matter?

After a time, I became aware that Harry was standing over me.

'Jakob.'

'What?'

'What are you doing?'

'Nothing.'

'Aren't you forgetting something?'

I raised my head a fraction, peered at him with one eye.

He jabbed a finger downwards. 'The tunnel. We can still get back. Get out.'

I had forgotten about the tunnel. I'd assumed it would have been closed. But I had no time to voice these suspicions before Harry was off, pushing through the door behind the bar that led to the back rooms and basement.

'It's this way, right?' he called back. I hurried to follow, catching up with him only at the bottom of the stairs. The basement was pitch black, but the bare lightbulbs flared into life when I hit the switch. A fine dust filled the air, settling on our clothes and giving Harry a ghostly complexion. He looked round expectantly at me and I pointed to the door on the right, at the end of the corridor. We made our way forwards.

Halfway down, Harry paused and nodded at something. On the hinges of one of the doors and on the nearby wall were crimson splatters. I reached out to touch. My fingertips came back red. We looked at each other then, and kept moving.

The door at the end opened into that familiar low-ceilinged room. I put my hand on Harry's shoulder and nodded towards the gaping hole in the floor. The light from the corridor did not penetrate far enough in to see it properly. I looked for a light switch, but remembered there wasn't one. Then I remembered the electric lamps that had been rigged up around the room, and I reached to down to plug them in.

A stern voice came from the darkness.

'Stop right there, Jakob.'

Hans.

He stepped out of the gloom. In one hand was a revolver. In the other, he held Dana tightly by the arm. Her eyes flared with fury. But she had been gagged with a dirty length of rope. There was a gash on her cheek that looked new.

The air seemed to go out of the room. Hans was half in shadows, his face barely visible. Just his mad, cold smile. Beside me, I felt Harry tense.

'Your little game is over,' Hans said. 'You are going to come with me. Maybe you'll get to see that *band* of yours. In prison. To think of everything I gave you, the opportunities … but no. No use. On the floor.'

He waved the revolver at me and I started to lower myself, slowly.

'As for you,' he said, turning to Harry. 'Your destiny is different, though just as clear.'

The revolver swung in Harry's direction. Hans' finger tightened on the trigger. I realised then he meant to shoot Harry. Hans was a killer. I lurched to my feet and moved in front of Harry. Dana shook her head, a tiny fraction that only I could see. A warning. I ignored her.

Hans laughed. 'You would die, here? For this – *American*?' He spat the word. 'I really did do a bad job with you. Very well. I will shoot both of you, and your bodies can rot in this pathetic tunnel.'

I should have been terrified, but though the gun was pointing at me now, I sensed a hesitation in him. Perhaps he still thought of me as his son. It was the only card I had.

'Dad, please. Let's be reasonable. There is no need for violence. You've won. We understand.' I tried to keep my tone calm, though daggers were twisting in my gut. I held his eyes and took a step towards him and to the left, trying to get his aim away from Harry.

One step was all it took.

Harry rushed past me, throwing himself forward, bundling into Dana and Hans.

A deafening crack ricocheted through the basement. All three collapsed in a tangle of limbs. I ran forwards to help, grabbed Dana's arm and pulled her out of the scrum.

Harry was on top of Hans. They were wrestling for the gun. But Harry was possessed by a cold fury. With one hand gripping Hans' wrist, he found a piece of rubble and swung it at Hans. It connected with Hans' head with a dull thud.

The gun skittered across the floor. Hans fell back, and Harry slumped forward onto him. Rolling away from Hans, he lay on the floor staring up at the ceiling and clutching his side.

He had taken a bullet. Blood was soaking his shirt red, sticking it to his skin.

'Harry!'

I leapt over. His eyes were open, blinking and unfocused. With her hands now free, Dana managed to undo the gag. She spat to clear her mouth.

'Get something to staunch the flow,' she said. 'Your sweater.' Then she switched to English and started talking to Harry fast, trying to keep his attention. I ripped my sweater off and held it over the bleeding hole in Harry's stomach.

'We need to get him to a hospital,' I said. 'I will call for an ambulance.'

But she saw the truth quicker than me.

'We can't, Jakob.' She took a quick glance at Hans' body. 'They'll arrest him. They'll arrest all of us. We have to go through.'

I knew she was right. But Harry couldn't walk, could barely stand, even with my support. Somehow, I managed to secure the body of my sweater over the wound by tying the arms tightly around him.

'Stay with us,' I said to him. 'We'll get through.'

If he couldn't walk, maybe he could at least crawl. Between us, we somehow managed to lower him awkwardly into the hole. I heard an intake of breath as he slumped forwards on to all fours. Dana had found a flashlight from somewhere and its beam highlighted a thick floating dust cloud and the rough walls of the tunnel propped up with wooden beams. Dana crawled ahead, then there was just enough space for me to put an arm around Harry and half crawl, half drag us both into the tunnel.

Harry whispered something I could just make out. 'I'm not going to make it,' he said.

'Yes ... you ... are.'

I gritted my teeth and pulled him onwards, his legs dragging heavily on the ground. I tried to ignore my claustrophobia, the feeling I was trapped in this tiny space. I knew I could do it. I had helped dig this tunnel and now I was going to get through it. All I could see was Dana, a couple of metres ahead in the blackness. I scraped my side painfully on a beam as the tunnel grew narrower. There were more wooden struts in this area and I realised that this must have been where the tunnel had collapsed previously. I remembered the stories I'd heard of escapes going wrong, tunnels collapsing. I tried to picture the map in my head – how far it was from Café Bruno, through No Man's Land, all the way to Harry's apartment block. But I had no real idea. All I could think of was the mountain of earth and stone above our heads. The cool, damp walls seemed to be closing in on us. Harry was getting heavier.

'Come *on*,' said Dana. 'Not far now.'

Then – behind us, I heard a sound. I looked back. There seemed to be a light at the eastern end of the tunnel. Voices. Had Hans regained consciousness? It sounded like he had back-up with him this time.

There was no time to think or plan.

'Take Harry,' I called to Dana up ahead.

'No,' she said. 'What are you going to do?'

'Take Harry,' I repeated. 'Keep going. There isn't time to explain.'

She hesitated for a second, but then started shuffling back towards us. I managed to transfer Harry so that his weight rested on her back and I heard them slowly shuffling forwards as I turned awkwardly to face our pursuers.

I crawled back ten metres, where it was dark apart from the faint light from what I assumed were flashlights. I examined each strut I passed, quickly assessing each in turn, looking for a possible weakness. If I could bring down the tunnel behind us, there would be no way through for whoever was coming after us. No way out for Gerold and the others either, but their fate was already sealed.

Finally, I noticed one that had bent out of shape a little

under the strain; there already seemed to be a slight crack in the wood. I lay on my back and kicked at it with the heel of my shoe, again and again. The shouts down the tunnel grew louder. They had heard me, and they called to me to stop, to remain where I was.

'Halt!' I shouted. 'Stop, or I'll shoot.' Maybe that would make them pause.

'Don't be stupid, Jakob.' The voice was still distant, but it was clearly Hans. 'You didn't even take the gun with you. I still have it here.'

Desperately, I kicked once more, and the strut came loose. I heard the groan of earth above. Turning quickly, I started scrambling back along the tunnel. Dust and small pebbles trickled from the ceiling. Then there was a horrible yawning sound, and the trickle turned into a torrent. Rocks struck my head, my shoulders, and I fell, scraping my chin on the cold floor. Behind me, the rumbling grew; time seemed to run in slow motion as finally the ceiling caved in with a crash that reverberated all around. Struggling to my knees, I set off again, crawling as quickly as I could down the narrow tunnel, straining my ears to listen for any sound of our pursuers.

I could just make out Dana's torch in the far distance. The tunnel started to slope upwards. It became harder and harder to keep going, as the dirt beneath me turned to mud.

Finally, I could see Dana and Harry up ahead. Here, the tunnel broke through into a brick-lined sewer. Harry was propped up against the wall. He was almost totally limp, his skin white. My sweater, damp with his blood, hung loose in his hand. She was stood ankle-deep in wastewater, battling to try and lift a large iron grate above her head.

I clambered down next to her and started to help. It was heavy, but I levered my legs against the wall and pushed until a small gap appeared, and I could use my hands to push the grate up and clear. Placing a hand on either side of the hole, I hauled myself up into the darkness. From the little light there was, I could make out a bare room, pipes running along the wall, a water tank. This had to be it. This had to be Harry's basement.

Somehow – my hands beneath his arms, Dana holding his legs – we managed to get Harry up. Dana followed, and we laid Harry on the floor. His breathing was shallow and uneven. My hands were sticky with his blood. I shoved the grate back in place.

Dana and I looked at one another, not quite believing. We were in the West.

HARRY

He has followed me around ever since it happened. The boy caught in the barbed wire. I can still hear the gun-shots.

At least I've made it further than he did. We got through the tunnel. Back to the West.

'We did it,' says Dana. 'We are in the American Sector now, yes?'

I nod, the only movement I can muster. Dana's face glows with relief. But then she looks down at me.

She moves the hair out of my eyes, the cold sweat making it cling to my forehead. She kisses my cheek and says, 'Harry, dearest Harry. I am sorry. You should never have been caught up in this.'

'I wanted to be,' I whisper, because it hurts to make any more effort.

Dana turns to Jakob and says, 'He needs help, fast. I will go. You stay here. Keep him talking. Don't let him lose consciousness.'

Then she disappears across the basement. For a moment I panic as I hear her rattling the door, but clearly the Hausmeister has grown negligent about locking up since I was last down here. There is nothing of value lying around, anyway. Dana's footsteps fade away as she runs to find help. I want to run too. Up the stairs, and all the way to my mom. I want to hug her and tell her I'm safe, that everything is going to be OK. I want to run but I can't. My legs are numb. Jakob takes off his jacket and scrunches it into a ball to make a pillow for my head. He stares at me. The colour has drained from his face. He looks like he's already seeing my ghost.

'Stay with me,' he says.

'Don't worry,' I say. 'I'm not going anywhere.' I try to laugh, but it hurts too much.

I guess my wound is bad, though Jakob tells me not to look. I can feel the dampness. I can feel my clothes sticking to my side.

'Harry,' he says. 'You were brilliant. You took Hans out.'

Did I really? Did I do that?

'I wish I'd killed him,' I say. And I mean it.

'I think he might be dead,' says Jakob quietly. 'I heard him in the tunnel, just before I managed to collapse it behind us.'

I close my eyes for a minute.

'Harry,' says Jakob, taking my hand. 'Are you OK?'

'Well,' I say, 'at least my nose doesn't hurt any more.'

'Harry, stay with me.'

Memories flash by from recent days, but they all feel like years ago, drifting further and further away.

'I remember,' I say, 'counting the steps in here. You remember, Jakob? I wrote to you about it. One, two, three, four. Pacing it out ... to the wall.'

I remember the letters, the smell of lemons.

'I was so stupid,' I say to Jakob. 'I just wanted to be a hero like The Fly.'

'I think you got your wish,' he says. 'You've done more than enough.'

But it's not enough. We are just three, and there are so many more that are stuck. Café Bruno is gone. The rest of The Stamp Collectors, gone.

People are beginning to gather in the basement, crowding in to see. Dana must have spread word through the apartment building. She probably knocked on every door believing there was safety in numbers.

Someone brings a blanket.

Someone tells me an ambulance has been called.

And then my mom's voice. 'Where is he? Where is he?'

I strain to look over to the door. I can see people shuffling out of the way to let her through.

When she sees me, she screams.

'Harry! Thank God you're alive!'

She bends down over me and puts her hands on my cheeks and kisses me on the forehead, over and over.

Tears burst from me, and I don't know if it's from being close to Mom again, or if it's the pain I feel from the bullet.

Mom squeezes my hand inside hers. Her sobs fill the basement. A neighbour reaches out. Puts a hand on her shoulder.

'Mom,' I say, 'I need to tell you about Dad.'

'Don't worry,' she says, 'we know. Oh, Harry, I'm so sorry, I can't believe I was that blind.'

I drift in and out of consciousness; the crowd of people seems to swirl, but I can feel my mom close by. She holds my hand in hers.

'They're coming,' she says, 'hold on, Harry, you're going to be OK. We're going to get you fixed up and then I'm taking you home. We're going home, Harry, back to Philadelphia.'

Then she turns and embraces Jakob, burying her face in his chest. He seems much older than that first time

I met him back in Café Bruno, when we were two lost boys playing at being men. And it's strange, but though Jakob and Dana look close to tears, there's something right about them both being here. The last of The Stamp Collectors. *Let them live*, I think to myself. *Let them know happiness.*

The basement is blurry now. Mom sings a lullaby, running her hands through my hair. I close my eyes for a minute and when I open them Jakob and Dana's faces are hovering above me. I want to speak to them, reassure them somehow that it's all right, but it takes every effort just to get a sentence out.

'Just think,' I say, 'you'll have a great story to tell. You'll have a great life here ... I know it.'

'You're speaking like it is the end,' says Dana.

'Maybe it is. It was a real adventure though, wasn't it?' I say, trying to find Jakob, reaching out for him. I hear a siren getting closer and then stopping. The crowd of people parts to let the stretcher through.

And I find myself wondering what The Fly would do.

Surely he wouldn't have died at the end of his own story ...

I feel Jakob's hand on my shoulder as the paramedics bustle nearby.

'Harry,' he says, '*my brother*.'

I look up and can see the tears running down his face.

'Don't worry,' I say, and my voice comes out as a whisper. 'It was worth it. You're free.'

THREE MONTHS LATER ...

I still find it strange walking through the streets of West Berlin like this. It is both as I imagined and not. It's certainly very different from the East. Faster and louder. As if the brightness has been turned up on all the colours. Huge, shiny American cars speed through the streets here. There are so many people from all over the world – American, British, French and more, all barging around in their fashionable clothes. I find it fascinating to eavesdrop on their conversations; half the voices you hear on the street are speaking a different language.

Dana and I are staying in rooms in a small, well-kept hotel in the American Sector, mostly populated by foreign bureaucrats. We spent our first few days being shuttled between various government buildings. We had interview after interview with different officials, American and

West German – a hundred different agencies that left us bewildered. Questions about Hans, the Funkhaus, the postcards. Everything, going over it again and again, until my mind whirled.

The people here seem fascinated by anything from the East, as if we are aliens from another planet. The western newspapers were full of our story. About the tunnel, about me and Dana and how young we both are. Most of all, though, they're interested in Harry. The all-American boy who broke into East Berlin to rescue two young victims of Communism. How he'd even been shot in the process but had made an almost miraculous recovery and was returning home as a hero. They didn't mention how difficult that recovery was. How Harry is still working hard to get well again.

We had visited Harry every day during his recovery, watching, relieved, as he'd slowly regained his strength. He had a room to himself up on the third floor, where his mother never left the chair by his side. It had been a couple of weeks before he had the energy to hold a conversation, but I never grew bored of sitting with him quietly. Later, I was always pleased when he asked me to help him sit up, or to take his arm for the short walk down the corridor to the toilet.

It was hard when the time came for him and his mother to leave. I think he was sad too, although obviously excited to be headed back to his family in Philadelphia. The journey home was the first time he had left the hospital in weeks. We promised to write to each other. We are good at that.

I linger as I walk past the supermarket. I was too nervous to eat breakfast this morning and now I'm feeling hungry. Looking through the window, I remember the first time Dana and I came across one of these places. We spent a whole afternoon just buying food we'd never tried. Peanut butter I loved, but Dana thought it was cloying and gross. We tried ten different kinds of chocolate bar – Milka, Hershey's, Kinder. We drank Kool-Aid and Coca-Cola. The thing that I was really excited about, though, was the bananas. Seeing them took me straight back to being a kid. The day my father – my real father – had come home one day with two of these strangely shaped yellow fruits, one each for me and Katrin. I can't remember ever seeing one in a shop in East Berlin after that, but here they were stacked as high as the potatoes and they tasted like heaven. I must have eaten at least half a dozen that first day, and I've got into the habit of having at least one or two a day ever since. So that's what freedom tastes like to me. Like bananas.

Those early days are already a bit of a haze. It's hard to keep track of time without the routine of school and the Funkhaus. I didn't expect to miss much about the East, but although it's poorer and you can never fully trust anyone, it was my home, and I understood it. West Berliners have a curtness to them. They're always rushing somewhere, and everyone else has to get out of the way. Still, I wouldn't go back.

I finally got my first letter from Harry a couple of days ago. It was strange to see his handwriting on the envelope but not smell that familiar scent of lemons.

Dear Jakob,

I hope you are enjoying West Berlin! I bet you're glad not to have to spend your afternoons in that dreary hospital with me any more. Have you started school yet? I hope you're making new friends. Please do write back and tell me about everything.

Things are going well here, if a little slowly. We are staying with my aunt, my mom's sister, while I get back on my feet. I'm able to move around a fair bit now. I made it out on to the porch today and sat watching the birds flittering around. It's so strange being back in Philly. Some things are so familiar from when I was a kid. The birdsong in the morning and the smell of my aunt's onion soup. But I feel like a completely different person.

Mom is doing well, or as well as can be expected. Sometimes at night, she comes to sit with me and tells me how sorry she is. But she seems a little happier with each day that passes. We helped my aunt cook dinner last night and managed to bake a very nice apple pie. Everybody agreed that Mom always did make the best desserts, which made her smile for the first time in ages.

I'm sorry that I had to leave before we found your mother, but I am sure that you will be reunited. Have you heard from Marie? I'm sure she'll be in touch soon. She must have seen our story in the papers. Have hope, Jakob.

Your friend,

Harry

Marie. How important she has become to me now, and yet, we've never even met.

Harry told me about Marie that first day we went to see him in the hospital. If I'm honest, she sounded too good to be true. A miraculous stranger who was going to bring my mother back to me after all these years. I tried not to let myself get carried away with Harry's enthusiasm. What did I really know about her? I didn't even really know for sure that my mother was in the West to be found. As time went by, my fears seemed to be realised. There was no word from Marie. No news about my mother.

Still, I couldn't stop them from appearing in my dreams. My mother and my sister. Sometimes we would be back in our childhood home, with my mother reading us a story or playing the violin while my father accompanied her on piano. But then, I would always wake up. And I'd be left on my own again.

Dana does her best to keep my spirits up, but the truth is, I've been very lonely here. Since Harry left, I spend a lot of my time in my hotel room. Whenever I do venture out for a walk, I have to be accompanied by an American guard. There's one behind me now, following discreetly about ten paces back.

Maybe it's because of the guards that I have a constant feeling of being watched. It's almost like being back in the East, never able to feel sure you aren't under surveillance. They won't tell us anything, but I can't help thinking that they wouldn't be keeping such close tabs on us unless we were still in some kind of danger.

I was watching a news broadcast the other day. They were covering an official statement by a high-up minister in the East, denying the rumours that there had been trades of prisoners with the West. I hoped that Harry's friend Dieter might be among those being returned to safety on this side of the Wall. But then a figure I recognised at the edge of the shot distracted me from this hopeful thought.

It couldn't be.

It was.

Hans.

The night of our escape came flooding back to me. The dread I felt as I heard Hans closing in on us down the tunnel. The noise as I brought the rubble down on top of him. I was sure that he couldn't have escaped. But there he was, standing among a small group of officials off to one side of the stage. As I watched, he looked up and straight into the camera with that familiar hard stare. A chill went down my spine. It was as if he was deliberately trying to let me know he was still alive. Then the show cut back to the presenter in the news studio and he was gone again. And I was left wondering if it had just been my imagination, or if maybe my adopted father wasn't finished with me.

*

I take the note out of my pocket and check the address I scribbled down. It seems almost unbelievable that it's this old apartment building, so like the one I lived in with the Eberhardts. It's so close to where I lived in the East too, if only the Wall hadn't come between us.

Marie finally wrote to me about a week ago, introducing herself and telling me she was coming back to Berlin, that she hoped we could meet. She apologised for not reaching out sooner, but it had not been easy to find out from the government where I had been staying. She'd call me, she wrote, when she got here. She hoped that she would have good news.

That call came this morning. And it was more than I could have imagined. She's found her. Marie has found my mother. And my sister, Katrin, too. They are waiting to see me, just on the other side of that door. I take a deep breath. I've spent so long imagining this reunion and now that it's almost here, I'm scared. I can feel myself shaking as I scan the windows for any movement.

I pause as I reach the door and then ring the bell. I can hear movement from inside, as if someone has been waiting on the other side. I hear urgent whispers and then the scraping of the latch. The door opens, and the woman on the other side is older than I remember her, her hair a little greyer, but there's no mistaking her face.

'Jakob!' she says, tears streaming down her cheeks.

'Hello, *Mami*.'

'MAXIMILLIAN JONES'

Welbeck Flame and Tibor Jones have collaborated to develop this book with a talented team of writers – G J Burgess, Michael Button and James Horrocks – who work with a dynamic and creative approach echoing the TV script-writing model. *The Boy Behind the Wall* and *Breaking Down The Wall* are both published under the fictional author name Maximillian Jones.

For more information and to download discussion notes for *The Boy Behind the Wall*, please visit: www.welbeckpublishing.com/trade

THE STORY CONTINUES ...

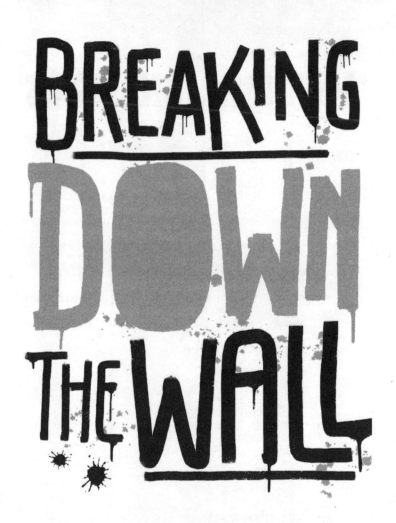

BREAKING DOWN THE WALL

AVAILABLE FROM SEPTEMBER 2022